The Law of Three

The Law of Three

By Caroline Rennie Pattison

A BOARDWALK BOOK
A MEMBER OF THE DUNDURN GROUP
TORONTO

Editor: Barry Jowett

Design: Alison Carr

Copy-editor: Andrea Waters

Printer: Webcom

Library and Archives Canada Cataloguing in Publication

Pattison, Caroline Rennie

The law of three / Caroline Rennie Pattison. (A Sarah Martin mystery)

ISBN 978-1-55002-733-4

    I. Title. II. Series: Pattison, Caroline Rennie. Sarah Martin mystery.

PS8631.A848L39 2008   jC813'.6   C2007-905729-2

1   2   3   4   5   11   10   09   08   07

Conseil des Arts du Canada   Canada Council for the Arts   ONTARIO ARTS COUNCIL   CONSEIL DES ARTS DE L'ONTARIO

We acknowledge the support of **The Canada Council for the Arts** and the **Ontario Arts Council** for our publishing program. We also acknowledge the financial support of the Government of Canada through the **Book Publishing Industry Development Program** and **The Association for the Export of Canadian Books**, and the Government of Ontario through the **Ontario Book Publishers Tax Credit** program, and the **Ontario Media Development Corporation**.

Printed and bound in Canada.

Printed on recycled paper.

www.dundurn.com

Dundurn Press	Gazelle Book Services Limited	Dundurn Press
3 Church Street, Suite 500	White Cross Mills	2250 Military Road
Toronto, Ontario, Canada	High Town, Lancaster, England	Tonawanda, NY
M5E 1M2	LA1 4XS	USA 14150

For Natasha and Jacob

This journal is the private property of
Sarah Elizabeth Martin,
student by profession, detective in training.

Psycho Girl

Date: Thursday, October 18
Location: School

Just when I was beginning to think that being forced to leave my old life to live in the sticks of Muskoka wasn't the end of the world after all, I had a nasty encounter with the school nutcase.

It happened while walking from homeroom to my first class. My new friends, Mindi Roberts and Stacey Payton, were telling me about some hot guy in their music class while Cori Stedman was shooting me daggers. Cori blames me for her family issues. It wasn't my fault her father got caught walking on the wrong side of the law. It can be tough being a ninth-grade detective.

Stacey had just said, "Hey, Mindi, Roy's hot, don't you think? I'll bet he asks you to the dance before the end of the day."

"Ugh! Leave my brother out of it!" I yelled, sidestepping towards Stacey as if to give her a shove. That was my first mistake. My geography text slid loose from the massive pile of books in my arms and fell to the floor with a smack that would deafen an elephant.

"Oh, crap," I mumbled.

Stacey laughed as I stopped and bent over to scoop up the fallen book. That was my second mistake. With the perfect timing of destiny — or fate, or whatever you want to call it — my fingertips barely touched the book when a fishnet stocking–clad leg plowed into my side. I was knocked down onto my hands and knees, a weight rolling over my back accompanied by a shriek that echoed all the way down the hall. Next thing I knew, I was lying on the hard floor with a strange-looking girl in a messy tangle of limbs.

"You tripped me!" she yelled, her eyes fiery.

"Sorry! I dropped my book," I explained, as we disentangled ourselves and struggled to our feet. "Are you okay?"

"No, I'm not okay!"

I clutched the offending book to my chest. The hallway, once teeming with bodies rushing off to their classes, was suddenly quiet and still.

"I'm sorry," I said again. "I didn't mean to ..." Then I stopped. I hadn't done anything wrong. She'd run into me.

I looked around at the crowd that had gathered, their faces curious. The girl glared at them through darkly lined eyes. Some people looked away or left. She did look a little scary. The rest of her face was as heavily made up as her eyes, leaving her true appearance largely up to the imagination. Her hair was dyed black and red and pulled into stubby pigtails exposing the shaved lower half of her scalp. A silver stud pierced the skin under her bottom lip, silver loops lined her ears, a silver-studded choker clasped her neck like a dog collar, and countless silver bracelets jangled at her wrist. She wore a short-sleeved, skin-tight black T-shirt that showed off the tattoos on her upper arms. Her legs, mostly visible due to the ultra micro miniskirt she was wearing, plunged into tall black boots.

Her eyes met mine. "What are you looking at?" she asked, sharply.

I turned away and mumbled yet another apology.

"What did you just call me?" she asked, taking a step closer.

Confused, all I could do was stutter. "I — uh —"

She leaned in and gave me a push. Not hard, but enough to force me to take a step backward. Someone gasped. Then another person yelled, "Cat fight!" and a crowd quickly gathered again.

"How do *you* like to be pushed?" the girl snarled, giving another shove, this one harder than the first. Again, I stumbled back a step.

I didn't think it was a good time to point out that I hadn't actually pushed her. That in fact, she was the one who'd fallen on top of me. If anything, I had more right to be angry than she did. I kept my mouth shut.

"Well? How do you like to be pushed?" she repeated. This time, I was ready for her. When she stepped in to give me another shove, I ducked to the side. She was caught off guard and actually stumbled when her hands glanced my arm, very nearly falling on her face yet again. A few giggles rippled through the crowd.

Not cool.

If she'd been mad before, she was steaming now. In hindsight, I should have just let her push me around a bit more. She would have gotten tired of it soon enough and it would have been over. But no. I had to go and cause her more embarrassment.

"You picked the wrong person to mess with," she said.

I held my hands up in protest. "I don't want to *mess* with you. This is just one big misunderstanding."

"Are you saying I'm stupid? That I don't *understand* what's going on?" she asked, her face darkening.

"No! I — uh …"

Before I could say anything more, she raised her left hand and crooked her first two fingers, pointing them at me. With her black-lined eyes narrowed, she mumbled strange words under her breath. Confused, I appealed to the crowd. Most people were staring in fascination. A few looked at me in sympathy.

"What are you doing?" I asked. Behind me, Mindi gasped.

The strange girl ignored me and carried on with her odd recital so that I wondered if she was ever going to stop. She did. But she wasn't done with me. She jabbed my chest with those long fingers, punctuating each jab with a word. "Never. Come. Near. Me. Again." Then, she stormed off, the crowd silently parting to let her through.

In a matter of seconds, the hall was loud and bustling once again with students on the move, streaming around me like water around a rock. The show was over.

"What just happened?" I asked.

"I think you were *cursed*!" said Stacey. She looked horrified.

I made a face. "Cursed? What do you mean?"

Mindi stepped closer and whispered, "That was *Garnet Hopper*."

"So?" I asked.

Stacey's eyes were wide. "I've heard about Garnet cursing people, but I've never actually seen it. Everyone says she's a *devil worshipper*, you know."

"Oh, come on!" I snapped.

"It's true," insisted Mindi. "She is. *And* her parents are in the Mafia." Stacey nodded furiously in agreement.

I stared at them. It seemed crazy, but they were serious. "Cori. You don't believe this stuff, do you?"

She nodded. "I heard her family's here in Muskoka because they're in a witness protection program. Her dad ratted out some of his Mafia friends a few years ago, and they've been after him ever since."

I shook my head. "It sounds like a load of stupid rumours."

"It's not, Sarah!" insisted Mindi. "Everybody says it's true."

"Look," added Stacey, "the bottom line is … everyone knows better than to get Garnet mad at them. In fact, most people just stay away from her."

"And you go and trip her!" added Mindi, alarmed.

"Of all people …" cried Stacey, looking like she was going to faint.

"I didn't do it on purpose!" I protested. "She fell over me!"

"Doesn't matter," said Cori. "She hates you now. You sure know how to pick your enemies."

The corners of her mouth twitched up ever so slightly. She was enjoying this.

"What exactly does it mean to be cursed by Garnet?" I asked Mindi at lunchtime as we headed for the cafeteria. "What do her curses do? Will my hair fall out? My teeth? Will I grow a third eye?"

Mindi frowned. "No! Uh … I'm not sure. You just don't want to get in Garnet Hopper's bad books."

"Too late." I snorted.

"Yeah," she agreed. "There's something else you

should know. Rumour has it that a couple of years ago, she was under investigation for murder."

"*What?*" I exploded.

"She wasn't convicted or anything …"

We arrived at the cafeteria. Every head turned our way as I walked self-consciously towards our usual table. It seemed to take forever to reach it. I swear I could hear my name being whispered all around me.

"Who did she supposedly kill?" I asked as soon as we sat down. I was hoping she'd say somebody's cat. It's not that I had anything against cats, but given the alternative …

She leaned close and answered quietly, "William Tremball."

"Please tell me that's a cat."

She just looked at me.

"Okay, I guess not." I stared down at my unopened lunch, speechless for once in my life.

After a moment, Mindi said, "No matter what you think about all the rumours, I think you need to lie low for the next little while and give her time to forget about you."

"You want me to go into hiding? Isn't that getting a little bit carried away?"

"Well … I don't think …"

Our conversation was interrupted by the noisy arrival of Roy, Chris, Cori, and Stacey. Mindi brightened at the sight of Roy. Inwardly, I groaned. Why did my best friend have to fall for my brother? What did I do so wrong in this life to deserve that?

The only good thing about Roy was that he brought Chris LeBlanc with him. Now *he* was worth paying attention to! Unfortunately, before I knew what was happening, Garnet and I were the talk of the table. Of course it was Roy who brought it up.

"Did you hear about the poor sap Garnet Hopper beat up and cursed this morning?" he asked. "I heard she was so scared she practically filled her pants."

"That was Sarah!" Cori squealed, only too eager to share the great news. Roy's mouth dropped open. Chris turned and stared at me like I was some kind of deformed bug.

"I did not get beat up!" I protested, sounding whiny even to my ears. "And I wasn't scared."

For the next eternity, I had to endure a reliving of my entire ordeal as told by Cori, Mindi, and Stacey. All the while, Roy and Chris were staring at me in morbid fascination. I should have just left. The only good thing about it was that I learned Chris went to the same elementary school as Garnet (though he was a grade behind). I pounced and ran an interrogation my father would be proud of.

"Is Garnet a devil worshipper?" I asked, cutting to the chase.

He nodded. "Yeah, I guess so. At least that's what people say."

"What do you say?"

He shrugged. "I remember what she was like before people said that about her. Back when we were in Muskoka Public, Garnet was always popular. In Grade 8, she bragged about going out with guys in high school. That's when she went out with Will Tremball."

"The guy she killed?" I asked.

Roy looked startled. "She killed someone?"

"Yeah. Goes right along with being a devil-worshipping, witness-protected Mafia member," I said.

Chris raised his eyebrows. "So you've heard all the stories."

I nodded. "What's true and what isn't?"

"I have no idea," he said. "All I know is that after Will drowned, I didn't see Garnet again until I started high school, two years later. By then, she was a lot different. Like she is now. And I hadn't seen her brother, Byron, either until this year, when he started coming here too."

"She has a brother? In Grade 9?" I turned to the girls. "Do you know him?"

"Yeah. He came to our school in Grade 7. He's not very friendly; I don't think he's ever said two words to me," said Mindi.

"His locker's right by mine," said Chris. "I've tried saying hi and talking to him, but he doesn't want to talk. He never used to be like that. He used to have friends, but now he's always by himself."

"Sounds like they've both changed," I said. "So,

William drowned?"

Chris nodded. "People say that Garnet just stood by and watched. That she didn't try to help him. The police did an investigation, and she was never arrested or anything. But it was enough to convince people that she did something wrong. There wasn't much official information, but Will's family would have been kept informed, and Will's brother, Nathan, has never kept it a secret that he believes Garnet killed his brother. He told everyone that the police didn't have enough evidence to press charges, even though they thought she was guilty. He's how most of the police information got leaked."

We were quiet for a moment. I tried to imagine what it would be like to watch someone drown and not try to save them. I couldn't.

Then Stacey brought up her favourite topic, the upcoming Halloween Dance. She's one of the organizers and, I'm sure, one of the keenest. I let their conversation drift around me, lost in my own thoughts.

I was late getting home due to basketball practice and was hoping to smell meatloaf coming from the kitchen. Instead, when I yanked open the door, my ears were assaulted by a screeching racket like I'd never heard before — well, not since my brother, Roy, made his first attempt at shaving. I dropped my jacket onto the floor and kicked off my shoes.

"Hey! What's going on?" I yelled.

"We're in the den, Sarah!" called Roy.

I burst into the room to find Mom kneeling on the floor, wrestling with a tiny, squirming pig who seemed to be doing its very best to free itself from her arms.

"I finally got my pet pig!" announced Mom, beaming. She blew a strand of hair out of her eyes and readjusted her hands around the frantic little bundle of joy.

"Why's it in the house?" I asked.

"Exactly!" said Dad, with a clap. "See, Gina, Sarah agrees with me: pigs belong outside."

"I told you, Edward," explained Mom. "I want a *house* pig. Amber's clean and hypoallergenic ..."

That's right, she said *hypoallergenic*.

"... so we wouldn't have to worry about Roy's allergies, and that's why she'd make such a good house pet," finished Mom.

"Wait a minute, don't drag me into this," said Roy. "I wanted a dog."

"So did I, son," said Dad with a nod.

Mom frowned. "You're both gone all day. I'm the one stuck here all alone day after day and I want a pig!" she said, her voice rising.

"So get a job," said Dad.

"There are no jobs! Don't you think I've tried?"

"Then at least get a pig that lives outside," said Roy.

"I wanted an indoor pig so I got an indoor pig!" said Mom, clenching her teeth. "Don't start telling me the kind of pet I should get when I need some company here at home."

Whoa. Roy needs to learn when to keep his mouth shut. I felt sorry for Mom; it was two against one.

"I think she's really cute. What's her name again?" I asked.

I couldn't hear Mom's answer over the sudden high-pitched squealing coming out of the cute little pig's mouth. Roy clamped hands over his ears.

Dad scowled. "Is she going to do that all the time?" he asked. "Like when we're trying to sleep?"

Mom set the pig down. Immediately, the noise stopped and its stumpy little legs went into high gear. Before you could say "Charlotte's Web!" it was snuffling and grunting behind the rocking chair in the far corner of the room, eyeing us all with suspicion.

"Isn't Amber the sweetest little thing?" Mom's eyes had a dreamy look as she gazed at her new pig.

I nodded. "Yeah. She just seems a little scared, that's all. So you can really keep a pig inside, huh?"

"Yes! I read all about pot-bellied pigs and they make really good indoor pets. You can take them for walks" — she gave Dad a look here — "just like a dog, and they can learn to use a litter box, just like a cat. You can train them."

Just then, Amber bumped into an end table and

Mom's favourite vase toppled and smashed onto the floor. Amber let loose with a round of squealing that would be worthy of the Queen of Pigs. Academy Award material.

Mom took off after her, crying, "It's okay, Amber. Relax. Everything's fine!" As if Amber understood English. Dad put his head in his hands and groaned.

It seemed like a good time to bring up the topic of Garnet Hopper. If anyone knew what to do, it was my dad, the OPP detective. "Dad, were you aware that an alleged murderer attends our high school?" I asked him.

He looked up. "An alleged ...? What are you talking about, Sarah?"

"I'm talking about Garnet Hopper. I just found out today that she's an alleged murderer, a devil worshipper, and a Mafia escapee in a witness protection program. *And* she goes to our high school every day. Roy and I don't feel safe," I explained.

"Hey! Leave me out of this. I wasn't the one who got beat up and cursed," said Roy.

Dad's eyes widened. "I think you'd better fill me in."

That's what I did.

When I was done, Dad look puzzled. "Let me get this straight. You don't feel safe at school because some girl pointed her fingers at you and said some mumbo-jumbo you couldn't even understand?"

"Everyone says she's a devil worshipper! She cursed me! Why shouldn't I feel threatened?"

He frowned. "What exactly do you think the curse is

going to do to you?"

"I have no idea, that's why I'm so worried. She's obviously capable of anything."

"Really. Roy? Do you know anything about this girl?" asked Dad.

"Sure. She's a freak of nature. She's nasty to just about everyone. And nobody talks to her," he said.

"Do you think Sarah should be worried?" he asked.

"Don't forget, Dad," I interrupted. "This girl has murdered — probably for less than what I did to her."

"Don't start jumping to conclusions," said Dad.

"I'm just saying that you might want to think about providing me with some protection or something ..."

He made a face. "Give me a break."

"So you don't care if I'm in danger every minute I'm at school?"

He just looked at me. Beside him, Roy smirked.

"I'm so lucky to have such a caring family!" I stomped out of the room.

Behind me, Roy was laughing.

I stomped harder.

Dealing with the Nutcase

Date: Friday, October 19
Location: School

This morning on the ride to school, I tried to stop thinking about Garnet Hopper, but the rhythmic sound of the bus wheels seemed to chant, "You're cursed! You're cursed!" so that I couldn't get her out of my head. What it boiled down to was that my personal safety — my *life* — depended on me and only me. My own family had abandoned me. I had to work alone.

I formulated a plan.

The first thing I did when I arrived at school was carry out step one. I headed for the office. A whoosh of cool air hit me as I pushed the door open and stepped inside. It was a cozy office — plants in the corners, cushy chairs, flowers. I joined the short line of students waiting at the counter and read the sign posted on the wall behind reception. It kindly requested all visitors to sign in and wear a name tag while in the school in order to ensure students' safety. I frowned. There was more concern for my safety in that little sign than there was in my entire family.

"May I help you?" asked the smiling woman behind the reception desk as I stepped forward.

"Sure. A friend of mine asked me if I could pick up a copy of her timetable," I said.

"Oh? Why would she do that?" she asked, her smile shrinking.

"She said something about making a change to her Teaching Assistant assignment," I said. "She needs to figure out different times …"

"She'll have to pick it up herself. I don't give out student timetables to just anyone."

"There's a problem with that. She can't get here herself, but she needs the timetable so she can get the changes made before losing her credit," I lied. The trick to effective lying was to sound as if you knew what you were talking about even if you didn't. I hoped that's what I was doing.

"Why can't she get here herself?" asked the secretary, with a raised eyebrow.

"Uh — she's writing a test first period and had to meet with her teacher first," I explained.

"Really?"

I shrugged. "It's a hard test."

She sighed. "What's her name?"

"Garnet Hopper."

She looked at me sharply and her mouth twisted.

After an agonizing moment when I was sure I'd be told to get lost, she turned to a computer and worked away at the keyboard. Next thing I knew, she'd printed off a timetable.

"You tell Garnet that next time she loses her timetable, she can come get a new one herself instead of sending someone else to do her dirty work," she said, no trace of a smile remaining.

I nodded and tried to look remorseful before skipping out of the office, proud of myself. I raced to the nearest bathroom and, once safely hidden away in a stall, examined the timetable. A short time later, I slipped into homeroom, Garnet's classes committed to memory.

After homeroom, I headed to geography class by routing through the math wing. Sure, it was slightly out of the way, but I needed the walk. Yeah, right. I happened to know Garnet would be heading for her math class at that exact time. Let's just say a little timetable told me so. But to my disappointment, I didn't even catch a glimpse of her. On a positive note, I wasn't actually late for geography class and only got told to stop running in the halls once.

While my geography teacher, Ms. Lytton, took attendance, I mentally plotted my route to English via the gymnasium. I snapped to attention when I heard her call out, "Byron Hopper!" There was a low answer from behind me. I swung around in my seat in disbelief, and there he was, the brother of the infamous Garnet. In my geography class this whole time. I'd never even noticed him!

He sat slouched behind his desk in the back row, a hood pulled down over his eyes. If he hadn't just answered to his name, I'd have thought he was catching a nap. What little I could see of his face told me nothing about him. Basically, he had a nose and a mouth, like everyone else on the planet. Nothing seemed twisted or out of place. How disappointing.

"Sarah Martin!" called Ms. Lytton. "Wakey, wakey!"

"Here!" I called, twisting back around to face the front of the room.

Throughout the long, boring class, I kept sneaking glances back at Byron, hoping to catch a better look at him. That stupid hood was up the whole time. And somehow, when the bell rang, he was the first out the door, so I didn't even get a look at him then. Talk about frustrating!

My detour by the gym to English class turned out to be nothing more than extra steps. Once again, I managed to miss Garnet. I wasn't going to let that discourage me, though. The plan was still young!

After wolfing down lunch, I ditched Mindi, Stacey, and Cori by making some lame excuse about finishing an overdue science assignment and headed for the library to carry out step two of my plan. The centre aisle of the school library was lined with computers angled so that teachers could keep an eye on what you were working on. I chose a computer furthest from the entrance, hoping to be left alone. What I was about to do was for my eyes only.

I logged in with my student number and thought about the Mafia rumour. I didn't really know much about the Mafia. That was about to change. I was deep into my research, finding articles and printing off the ones that I wanted to read more carefully later, when a familiar voice from behind took me by surprise.

"There you are!"

I hit the minimize icon and spun around guiltily. Mindi and Stacey were heading straight for me.

"Hey, guys. What's up?" I asked, trying to look happy to see them.

"We wondered if you were done your science yet. Cori didn't think it would take you very long," said Stacey.

Great. Cori, the bigmouth, made it her business to judge how long my assignment should take me. I mentally kicked myself in the butt for choosing science; I should have realized I had a mole in that class.

"Come watch the boys' volleyball tournament with us," said Mindi.

"There are five other schools here. That's a lot of boys to watch," added Stacey, with a grin.

It did sound fun. However, I was in the middle of

an investigation. So, in an amazing act of self-control, I opened my mouth to say no, only to be interrupted by the science mole herself, Cori.

"Here's the stuff you printed, Sarah." She held up a bunch of papers just beyond my reach, for the entire world to see. "I was over there talking to Tony ..." She smiled and gave a little wave to a boy sitting by the printer.

He'd been staring at Cori and wearing a stupid lopsided grin. He waved back, face reddening. Jeesh! Were there any boys out there resistant to Cori's looks? Didn't anyone care about personality? Take me, for example, I've got tons of personality. But you'd never catch a guy staring at me like that. Sigh. Maybe I should consider plastic surgery.

"... and he noticed these printouts mixed in with his. They had your header on them. So he asked me, 'Who's this Sarah kid and why's she so interested in the Mafia?' I told him how you're a little different, but harmless, and that I'd give them to you." She handed over the papers with a flourish, wearing a bright smile. The one she used when attempting to humiliate a fellow human being.

Mindi looked puzzled. "The Mafia? I thought you were doing your science homework?"

"I was. Uh ... I just thought ... since I was here ... that I'd find out some things about the Mafia," I explained.

"Why?" asked Stacey, looking as puzzled as Mindi.

"You told me all about how Garnet's family is either part of the Mafia or hiding out from them, so I thought it might be a good idea to get to know what I'd gotten myself into," I explained.

"What you'd gotten yourself into? You mean you weren't really doing science homework?" said Stacey.

I reddened.

"Why didn't you just tell us you wanted to research the Mafia?" asked Mindi.

I shrugged and felt foolish. "I guess I thought you'd think I was nuts."

"You are nuts," said Cori, making a face.

Mindi frowned. "You're getting too worried about Garnet. I told you to just lie low and she'd forget all about you."

"You also told me she's a murderer! Not to mention all those stories about her family. Don't you want to know the truth?" I asked.

It was a consensus. None of them cared about the truth.

"I just wanted to know who I've made enemies with, that's all," I said quietly, following them out of the library.

My notes from the articles I printed about the Mafia before being unexpectedly interrupted ...

- The Mafia was a secret society formed in the mid-nineteenth century in Sicily. It moved into the United States during the late nineteenth century through Italian immigration. Today, the Mafia is the most powerful criminal organization operating in the United States.

- The Mafia has been in Canada since the immigration after the Second World War, mainly in large city areas like Montreal, Toronto, Hamilton, and Windsor. Their criminal activities include drug dealing, money laundering, extortion, and murder.

- The "Global Mafia" is the "world's fastest growing industry" with profits up to $1 trillion.

- The Mafia is organized by "families." Each family is controlled by a "Don" or "Boss." The "Underboss" is appointed by the Don and is second-in-command. The "Consigliere" is the family advisor. And the "Capo" or "Captain" is in charge of a "crew." A family usually has four to six crews, each made up of twenty to thirty "Soldiers" who conduct the actual operations. "Soldiers" are "made members" of the family and started as "Associates" who've proven themselves.

- The term "mafia" is also used to describe any large group of people involved in organized crime.

Wow! Could there really be people involved in the Mafia right here in Muskoka? Cool.

The Investigation Continues

Date: Sunday, October 21
Location: The Town Library

Dad dropped me off at the town library on his way to the hardware store this afternoon. My plan was to look up back copies of local newspapers to see if I could find any information about William Tremball's death. Of course, when Dad asked me why I wanted to go to the library, I let him know.

"I'm trying to save my life," I said.

"What?" He looked startled.

"I'm trying to save my life."

Huge sigh. "What are you talking about?"

"Well, my *father*, who so happens to be an OPP detective, knows more than he's saying about an old case involving a student who attends the same school as his only daughter. Did I mention this was a *murder* investigation? And that the alleged murderer is the very same person who recently put a fatal devil's curse on the same only daughter? And since my *father* thinks it's not worthwhile to protect his own daughter from certain danger, possibly death, then I have to take care of myself. I have to investigate this old case, against all odds, all alone. Without my uncaring, unloving father's help."

He sighed and didn't ask me any more questions. In front of the library, he grunted something about being back within an hour, then drove off, tires squealing.

The library was bright and cheery, in a hushed sort of way. It was bigger than I expected for a small town; computers were set up at various stations throughout, and a few glassed-in rooms lined the wall to my right. I had no idea where to start, so I went directly to the librarian behind the long front counter and asked if they kept copies of the local newspapers from as far back as two and a half years ago. They did — on *microfilm*. Since that was a new concept to me, she led me to one of those glassed-in rooms, sat me down in front of an archaic-looking machine, and showed me how to use it. She then directed me to catalogued stacks and explained which of the local newspapers were archived. I thanked her enthusiastically. Funny how a perfect stranger can be more helpful than my dear old dad.

Left on my own, I selected several films of archived newspapers to search. In spite of being a beginner klutz when it came to using the microfilm, I did eventually find what I was looking for. The first article had this headline: "Tragic death of young teen shocks community." Sure enough, the "young teen" was none other than William

Tremball. I rocked back in my seat, taken aback. He really existed. And he really died. I guess some part of me had been hoping that the student's death, and therefore Garnet's murder rap, was more rural myth than fact.

Excited by my find, I tracked down the ultra-helpful librarian and got her to show me how to print off the article. Once again, she didn't disappoint. Knowing that I had the right time frame, I kept working my way through the old newspapers, looking for anything that might be about William's death. I found a second article: "Young teen's drowning not accidental?" I felt like singing; I was such a good detective!

I was collecting my printouts when I sensed a large hulking body behind me.

"Did you find what you were looking for, Sherlock?" asked Dad.

I proudly handed the articles over to him. "Mission accomplished." He read through them. "Well?" I asked when he passed them back.

"Well what?"

"Don't you have anything to say?"

"About ...?"

"*Garnet Hopper*!" I was getting frustrated. "I told you she's an alleged murderer! And now I have it all there, in black and white."

He arched an eyebrow at me. "All you have here is confirmation that William Tremball died in a tragic drowning accident and that a friend of his had the misfortune of being with him when it occurred."

"Really?"

"Don't you think so yourself?" he asked, looking surprised.

"Uh … I haven't actually read the articles yet."

"Then you have no idea what you have there."

"Uh … no."

He hitched up his belt and headed for the door. "I guess you've got some reading to do. You might have wanted to check out the evidence, or should I say lack of evidence, before sharing it with your Superior Officer. By the way, that's S.O. for short," he called back over his shoulder.

"S.O. for show-off," I murmured under my breath.

"I heard that."

GRRRRR!

When we got home, I ran to the privacy of my room and read each of the articles thoroughly. To my disappointment, Dad was right. The articles didn't give me the cold, solid evidence I needed to confirm Garnet's status of alleged murderer. Obviously, there had been an investigation around William's death, but the friend with him was not identified as Garnet.

I still had so many questions. If Garnet was the friend on the boat with William that day, and I think she was, did she try to save him? Or did something more sinister happen? Why did the autopsy and forensics investigations take so long? Why was the eyewitness (Garnet) repeatedly questioned? What didn't add up for the investigating officers? Why wasn't anybody (Garnet) charged?

I want to know!

Tragic death of young teen shocks community
June 13

BRACEBRIDGE — William Tremball, age 14, drowned in Lake Muskoka, June 12. He and a friend were boating on the lake when a fast-moving storm front swept through the area. He died while attempting to swim through the turbulent water back to his boat.

The two inexperienced boaters hadn't ensured that the anchor was properly secured. As a result, the boat had drifted dangerously far. Eventually, William's friend, an accomplished swimmer, was successful in reaching the boat. Numerous efforts were made to help William do likewise, but to no avail.

William Tremball, son of Gregory and Nancy Tremball, brother to Nathan, was a kind and talented young man who will be sorely missed by his family and friends. Funeral services will be held this Saturday, June 19, at the United Church and Cemetery on Eagle Road, Bracebridge, Ontario.

Young teen's drowning not accidental?
June 18

BRACEBRIDGE — Was William Tremball's recent tragic drowning an accident?

That is the question now being asked, according to reliable sources. Reportedly, William's family is questioning the length of time it is taking for autopsy and forensic testing results to be finalized, thereby allowing the release of William's body for burial. In addition, the key eyewitness to William's death has been repeatedly questioned about the details of events leading up to and resulting in his drowning.

"My William was cut off in the prime of his life," sobbed his devastated mother. "If his death wasn't an accident, then the person responsible needs to be punished to the fullest extent of the law — no matter what age they are!"

Is this a question of punishment? Not according to Bracebridge Detachment Chief of Police Thomas Harvey. "Innocent until proven guilty. There's no question of punishment for someone who is innocent. The last thing we need is for people to jump to conclusions. Routine questioning procedures are being followed and that's it."

Accidental or otherwise? The investigation, at this point, is ongoing and has yet to decide.

Investigation Full Steam Ahead!

Date: Wednesday, October 24
Location: School

My investigation had not one but two major breakthroughs today! One involving Garnet, the other involving her strange little brother, Byron.

The excitement started when my drama teacher set us free a few minutes early. I bolted for the science wing, and by the time the bell rang, I was casually leaning against a locker that gave me a plain view of Room 121, Garnet's class. Students escaped in a steady stream, chatting loudly. There was a noticeable empty space around Garnet as she walked; no one got too close to her.

I followed her down the hall, keeping an appropriate distance behind so as to avoid detection, when she suddenly stopped in her tracks. I'd allowed myself to get a mere three students behind before I noticed — not an acceptable distance at all! I strained to see what was going on over the heads in front of me.

A tall boy with wavy reddish brown hair and a face

full of freckles had blocked Garnet's path. I recognized him from the boys' volleyball team. Garnet tried to move around him; he wouldn't let her, grinning maliciously. Did he have a death wish?

"Get out of my way, Nathan!" said Garnet, after her third attempt to pass.

"What if I don't? Will you put a spell on me?" he asked, with an unattractive sneer.

"Is that what you want?" she asked darkly.

"What's good for my brother is good for me!" He took a step forward so that he was only inches from her face.

"Back off, Nathan!" yelled Garnet.

"What's the matter, Garnet? J.D. not here to protect you?"

"I don't need anyone to protect me. I can take care of myself," she snapped.

A girl with short brown hair and dark eyes stepped out from behind Nathan and took his arm. "Forget about her, Nathan, let's get to class," she said, leading him away.

As they passed, he shot Garnet a withering look and said, "Leanne, can you believe they let people like *her* walk the halls of this school?"

Garnet didn't respond, her face twisted in anger.

Talk about being in the right place at the right time! To catch Nathan Tremball in nasty conversation with Garnet Hopper, his brother's alleged murderer. I turned to head to science class and bumped into Cori.

"Happy now?" she asked.

"What do you mean?"

"You must have enjoyed that little encounter between Nathan and Garnet; after all, isn't that why you've been following her around everywhere?"

"Well, I wouldn't say that I actually *enjoyed* it …"

"Right." She swung around and walked away.

I made a face at her back.

After science class, Cori escorted me to the cafeteria where we were meeting Stacey and Mindi for lunch, making the possibility of taking a detour to the tech wing (where Garnet would be) impossible. It was like having a babysitter or an impossibly nosy neighbour looking over your shoulder. I actually looked forward to geography class where I'd be Cori-free! And geography's my least favourite subject. However, my good feelings towards geography were short-lived. Ms. Lytton gave out the dreaded independent project. The one that'll generate fifty percent of everyone's final mark. In my case, a failing mark.

I sighed and looked down at the project description, expecting the worst. I wasn't disappointed. I forced myself to read through the requirements. Was it me or was it written in Greek? I gave up trying to decipher it and tried to focus on Ms. Lytton, who was describing the expectations in more detail. They still didn't make any sense, so I stopped listening. I was going to fail.

When the bell finally rang, I stood up, ready to bolt.

"Sarah, may I see you for a few minutes, please?"

I stopped mid-stride. It was Ms. Lytton. Reluctantly, I turned and headed back to her desk, fighting against the flow of students rushing to the door.

"Have a seat," she said, gesturing to a chair by her desk. I sat.

"I sense that you're feeling a little overwhelmed by this project," she said, looking sympathetic.

I shrugged. "A little."

"I've noticed that you struggle with the assignments. Have you considered getting a tutor?" she asked.

I sank further into the seat. "No, I can do it," I said, quietly. A tutor wouldn't be worth Roy's teasing.

"Hmmm." She stared at me a moment, looking thoughtful. "What about a partner for the project, then? Would that be helpful?"

"But I thought it was supposed to be an independent project?" I asked.

"Actually, I'm planning to make partnering a requirement. I'm sure many people will be glad to hear that."

"Oh … okay."

"Is there anyone you'd like to work with?" she asked.

"I don't really know too many people in the class yet," I said. Suddenly, it hit me. This was a golden opportunity! "Except … Byron Hopper seems pretty smart. Maybe I should be his partner," I said. It was true. Over the past couple of days, I'd observed him in class. He didn't do much to participate, but when he was asked a question, he always knew the answer. And he always seemed to have his homework done.

Ms. Lytton's eyebrows lifted. "Byron, huh?" She tilted her head and considered it. "You know, that might just be a good arrangement for both of you," she said. "I'll let him know tomorrow that he'll be working with you."

"Uh, shouldn't we ask him first?"

"Oh, no. I'll tell him. Now, you'd better get off to your next class before you're late."

I gathered up my books and tried hard not to skip out of the room. Not only was I going to be saved in geography, but I was also going to be able to dig deep into the Hopper family! There'll be no secrets by the time I get through with them!

Tonight, I did some research into the witness protection program, just in case that rumour is true ...

- The witness protection program in Canada is administered by the Commissioner of the RCMP (Royal Canadian Mounted Police).
- A "witness" is someone who gives or agrees to give information or evidence, or who participates or agrees to participate in a matter relating to an investigation or the prosecution of an offence. A witness may also be any person who, because of their relationship to the witness, also needs protection.
- As part of this protection program, a person may be: relocated; provided a place to live; given a new identity; provided with counselling; and provided with financial support. The goal is to ensure the person's safety, as well as to help them re-establish themselves and eventually become self-sufficient.
- Usually, once people are in the program, they are in it for life. Most protection agreements are reviewed at least every six months. The Commissioner may end the program if the witness does not fulfill their obligations, e.g. to provide the agreed-upon information. Some people refuse the protection because of its restrictiveness and/or their unwillingness to

leave their extended families.

- It is an offence to knowingly expose information about a person in the program or who is no longer in the program.

So, could this be the real deal with the Hoppers? Have they been relocated and given new names because they were witnesses who agreed to give information? If so, I wouldn't even be able to tell anyone.

Independent Study with Partners

Date: Thursday, October 25
Location: School

Sometimes it only takes a few words to totally change your life, such as "Sarah Martin and Byron Hopper, you'll be working together." True to her word, Ms. Lytton established partners for the so-called independent project, and when Byron and I were announced as partners, I turned around to see his reaction. He sat motionless. Some of the other students giggled a little, and the girl sitting to my right gave me a sympathetic look and leaned closer. "Maybe you can get your partner changed," she whispered, "so you don't have to work with that *freak*!"

After the bell rang, I gathered up my books and took off after Byron, who was already heading out the door in front of me. I'm not usually that keen to start working on projects, but I was eager to start this one. And not because I suddenly liked geography.

"Byron!" I called. He kept walking. I called again. Still, he walked. Was he deaf? "Byron!" I called again, louder. Just about everyone turned around. Everyone but Byron. I jogged up beside him and touched his arm. He turned, scowling at me.

"What do you want?" he asked.

"I thought we should set up a time to start working on our project."

"Really."

"Well, yeah. It looks hard. We should probably start working on it pretty soon."

"I don't do partners."

He walked away, leaving me standing there like an idiot. Why did I want to work with this guy? Oh yeah, his family's weird and his sister might have killed someone. Right. I made a face at his retreating back just as Stacey swept by, caught in the stream of students surging down the hall. She looked alarmed.

"Hey, Stacey!" I called. But it was too late. She was gone.

The next time I saw Stacey was after school in the change room with Mindi. We were getting ready for our basketball game.

"Why did I see you talking to Byron Hopper?" she asked.

"She's probably using him to learn more about Garnet. Am I right, Sarah?" asked Mindi, tossing back a strand of bronze hair.

I nodded sheepishly. "Sort of."

Stacey looked startled. "First you're researching the Mafia, then you're following Garnet around, and now you're going after her brother? What's going on?"

"I'm not exactly going after her brother," I explained. "The teacher assigned us to work on a geography project together. It has nothing to do with Garnet."

"Right," said Mindi.

"If I were you, I'd forget all about the Hoppers. I wouldn't chase them around. They're dangerous," said Stacey.

I frowned. "But you don't even know if any of the stories about them are true."

Mindi leaned closer, her voice low. "Sarah, at least some of it's got to be true. Do you know that when there's been an accident or when something bad happens, some people will swear it was because of the Hoppers? They just can't prove it."

"That's right. Garnet's not the only one to look out for. Stay away from Byron, too," Stacey added. "It's not *just* for your safety. Do you want people to start thinking you like the guy? You're new around here; you don't want people to start thinking you're associating with the Hoppers."

To my alarm, Mindi was nodding in agreement. "Social suicide," she said.

My stomach lurched. I hadn't thought of it like that. What had I gotten myself into? I'd been so interested in getting to know more about the Hoppers, I hadn't thought about how hanging around with Byron would look to other people. Why didn't I keep my mouth shut and let Ms. Lytton pick my partner for me? Darn my impulsiveness!

"Just tell Lytton that you tried but you can't work with Byron," said Stacey.

I chewed on my bottom lip. Could I do that? After asking for him as a partner? I could tell her the truth: that he was rude and didn't want to work with me.

"Okay, I guess I can talk to her," I agreed.

"That's the first sensible thing I've heard you say all day," said Stacey, patting my back.

The Mystery Boy

Date: Friday, October 26
Location: School

I'm exhausted. I spent the entire night tossing and turning. If I wasn't dreaming of Garnet with fangs, snarling at me while shaking a devil's trident, then it was of Byron brandishing a bloody axe, holding a dead kitten. I had to get a grip! I pulled myself together over breakfast, with Amber curled at my feet. Since she's stopped bringing down the walls with her squealing, I really like having her around. And I'm pretty sure I'm her favourite Martin.

In geography class, Ms. Lytton gave us time to work with our partners. I stood up and braced myself for Mr. Unfriendly Hopper. He was slouched in his seat, an open textbook perched on his desk. I studied him and wondered if he was packing. After all, his family was supposedly involved in organized crime. A strand of long brown hair escaped his hood and fell over one eye. He swiped at it only to have it fall back in place. He had no intention of getting up to work with me. I sighed and walked over.

"Hey," I greeted, dropping my notebook and pen onto the desk.

He grunted and swiped at that hair again. I fought the urge to push his hood back and make him sit up. Instead, I peered into his open geography book.

"So that's what the inside of the textbook looks like," I said, as a joke. Humour often works to break the ice, I find. At least with normal people.

"I already told you, I prefer to work alone," he grunted.

"Hey, me too, but according to Ms. Lytton, we're stuck with each other," I said, trying to sound cheerful. "So, fill me in. What do we have to do?"

He tore his eyes away from his book at last and glared at me. "Don't you get it? We're going to do our independent study, *independently*," he stated flatly. His eyes were dull, with no sparkle of life under the shade of his hood. Kinda spooky, like his sister.

"Duh!" I forced a laugh and attempted to shake off the creeps he was giving me. "What I meant was, what parts of the project do you want *me* to do? You're the geography expert. I'm going to let you take the lead on this one."

He snorted. "You mean you want me to do it all and you'll just sign your name to it?"

I screwed up my face. Where did he get *that*? "No,

that's not what I meant," I explained. "I just thought that since you're apparently the brains of this outfit, you're the better one to make the decisions and I'll do what I have to do. Jeesh! Don't be so touchy!"

His face relaxed slightly. Very slightly. We sat in silence for a long moment. I tried to focus on the words in the project description. They weren't any more enlightening today than they were yesterday, so I gave up and studied Byron instead. He leaned over his papers, pen in hand, engrossed in his own work.

Just when I thought he'd forgotten about me, he spoke. "If you insist on sitting there —"

"If I *insist*?"

"— this is how it's going to be. First of all, stop staring at me."

"I'm not staring at you," I protested.

"You're staring. Stop it." He pushed over the assignment sheet. How could he have known I was staring? Did he have eyes on the top of his head or something?

"You're doing it again," he warned.

I forced my eyes to look down at the sheet he'd given me.

"I divvied the project up into parts. I starred the things we'll have to do together. The other stuff we can just do separately. I circled the easiest ones for you to do by yourself. Do you think you can handle them?" he asked with a sneer.

"Yes," I snapped.

Then I looked down at the circled items and gulped. Well, they weren't too bad. Better than the whole assignment, right? I read the starred items, the ones we had to do together. One was to prepare and deliver a role play demonstrating the impact of technological change on a community planning project. (What?) The other was to create an infomercial that identified and analyzed the positive and negative impacts on people and the environment of the manufacture, transportation to market, and consumption of selected products. (Again, what?)

I couldn't help it, I groaned. Out loud. To get this done, Byron and I would have to spend a lot of time together. What had I gotten myself into? I sneaked a glance at him, risking another staring accusation. He looked miserable. At least we agreed on something. I scanned the other choices. I didn't see anything any easier than what he'd picked. It was still all Greek to me.

I threw up my hands in surrender. "Let's figure out how we're going to get all this done over the next three weeks."

We spent the rest of the class scheduling work sessions for the starred items. The fact that we had to manoeuvre around my Monday and Wednesday basketball practices and Thursday games annoyed him tremendously; I was nothing but a pain. Finally, we settled on Tuesdays after school and Sunday afternoons in the town library. He grudgingly showed me the sections of the textbook that would help me with my circled items and wrote out the page numbers with his neat, meticulous printing.

We were saved by the bell. He bolted from class, eager to be rid of me. I took my time gathering together my things. Clearly, working with Byron wasn't going to be worth it; I wasn't going to learn anything more about Garnet from him. I approached Ms. Lytton.

"Everything okay, Sarah?" she asked.

"Um … no. Not really. I think working with Byron is going to be a problem for me," I said.

"Oh? Why's that?"

"He's — uh — difficult to get along with."

"I see." She cleared her throat. "Just so you know, Sarah, Byron's already been to see me about not wanting to work with you."

"Oh," I said, with a start.

"And I told him exactly what I'm about to tell you," she continued. "Anyone can work with anyone for a specified period of time. In fact, it's a life skill to be able to work cooperatively with someone who may not necessarily be your friend."

Did she just say that working with Byron would be a life skill? Shouldn't she have said a *life-threatening* skill? "So, I can't change partners?" I asked, crestfallen.

She looked at me for a moment. I'd never noticed before how frog-like her eyes were. "Tell me more about why you want to."

"Okay. I tried to talk to him yesterday about the

project and he was just rude to me. He told me he didn't want to work together. We're not going to be able to get along," I explained.

She frowned. "Sarah, I have a feeling that he'll get better to work with over time. You just have to get to know him a little."

"That's fine, but what if *he* doesn't want to get to know *me*?" I persisted. "He was rude and unfriendly for no reason. I know I need to work with someone to get this project done, but if I'm partnered with him, I might as well be on my own."

"Yes, you'll need to work with someone in order to be successful with this project. That was the main reason I agreed to put you with Byron when you asked. He's very good in geography. In fact, I told him so when he came to see me. I told him he'd be a good tutor for you and that helping you would be good for him."

"You said that?" I asked. Great! Now I'm Byron's charity case and he knows it!

She nodded. "It's okay, Sarah. Everyone needs help sometimes. We can't be good at everything."

And that was supposed to make me feel better?

She continued. "Now, I'm going to say the same thing to you that I said to him. I want you to give it a week and see if you two can work out an understanding. If you really can't after trying for a week, come back together and see me. Okay?"

I reluctantly agreed; what choice did I have? Inside,

I was groaning. What a disaster. A disaster of my own making! I was stuck being partners with the rudest person I'd ever met all because I was curious about his family!

What was wrong with me?

Amber's Demolition

Date: Saturday, October 27
Location: Mr. Braemarie's Farmhouse and Home

Mindi and I spent the afternoon at Mr. Braemarie's farmhouse today. Mr. Braemarie is Mindi's mom's boyfriend. His farmhouse is out in the boonies, too; a mere bike ride away. Since becoming Mindi's friend, I've been riding his horses and helping Mindi take care of them. In fact, hanging out with Mindi at the farmhouse was the one thing that made my move to Muskoka bearable when I first arrived. I've become a little horse crazy. Mom says it's better than being boy crazy. Little does she know, I can be both.

We were walking our horses, cooling them down after our ride, when Mindi said, "I still can't believe Lytton's making you work with Byron after both of you asked to get out of it."

"I know. At least he hasn't had me knocked off yet," I said.

She chuckled. "Seriously. How terrible is it, working with him?"

"Let's just say he isn't Prince Charming and he'll never win Mr. Congeniality," I said with a grimace.

"Why don't you just work by yourself and let Ms. Lytton think you're working together?"

"I would if I could, but it's a massive project and I'm a huge geography dunce." I sighed. "So, I guess I'll just have to put up with him. At least for a week. Hopefully, I'll survive." After a moment, I added, "You know, as irritating as he is, I get the impression that he's a very unhappy person."

"No!" Mindi snorted sarcastically.

"I mean, maybe he just needs someone to be nice to him."

"Please tell me you don't plan to be that someone."

I paused. "No. I'll leave that for some other poor sap, I guess. Although —"

"Don't say it!"

"— I still want to get to the real story of his family and put an end to all the rumours."

Mindi made a face. "Why? Who cares?"

Before I could answer, a familiar and unwelcome voice yelled, "Hey! You guys going to ride all day or what?"

Mindi's face lit up. "Oh, Roy's here." Immediately, she headed towards him.

"*Oh, Roy's here*," I mimicked under my breath before following.

Roy swung up onto the fence and sat on the top rail. "What's going on?"

"Sarah and I were just talking about the Hoppers," said Mindi. I groaned. Why would she tell him that?

Roy glared at me. "Sarah, let it go. You don't want to get mixed up with that family. They're not worth it. Find another mystery to solve."

"What are you doing here, Roy? Don't you have any friends of your own?" I asked.

"He's okay, Sarah. We're done riding, anyway," said Mindi, smiling at Roy.

He winked at her. She giggled.

Oh, brother.

Back at home, Roy and I raced our bikes up the driveway, dropped them at the garage, and sprinted to the porch, elbow to elbow. I took the stairs two at a time and burst through the door just ahead of him.

"I win!"

"Cheater!" he yelled. "You can't push me out of the way."

"You're just mad because you didn't push me out of the way first!" I yelled back.

"I don't cheat!"

"Hah!"

Then he was looking over my shoulder. "What's wrong, Mom?"

I whirled around, alarmed. Mom stood in the hall behind us. Her face was red, her eyes wet. "Amber's lost!" she cried. "She must have gotten outside somehow, but I've looked everywhere and she's nowhere in sight."

"Well, geez, Mom, maybe if you let her outside more often, like most pigs, she wouldn't get lost so easily," said Roy. "We'll look for her after dinner, right, Sarah? Ow!"

I'd elbowed him in the ribs for being so insensitive. "Don't worry, Mom, we'll help you find her. Dinner can wait. I'm sure Roy won't starve to death anytime soon — unfortunately."

I figured, how hard could it be to find a pig? Well, holy cow! We ended up searching for ages; that darn pig knew how to get lost! We looked all around the outside of the house, including some of the dense woods that surround our huge yard. We searched the area behind the garage where Mom had set up an outdoor piggy playground. Yes, that's what she called it, an outdoor piggy playground. We walked up and down the street, calling her name and listening for any of the usual squeals we'd come to expect from her. Nothing.

When Dad got home from work, he joined the search. We didn't have any better luck. We finally had to face the horrible possibilities. Of those horrible possibilities, the best-case scenario was that Amber had wandered too far and would eventually find her way home when she got hungry. However, Mom worried that she had been hit by a car or that someone might have pignapped her. I pointed out that nobody ever comes way out here to no man's land, and even if they did, why would they steal our pig? But she wasn't reassured. Apparently, pot-bellied pigs are a hot item.

By that time, we were starving. I ran up to my room to change, taking the stairs two at a time. I stopped short when I heard muffled noises coming from inside my room. Was Roy in there planning to jump out at me when I opened the door? He liked to play jokes like that every once in a while. I listened for a second or two longer before throwing open the door to startle him and backfire his plans to scare me.

Turned out, the joke was on me after all. My room was a complete disaster; World War Three had arrived. My unmade bed had been rumpled to the point where the bare mattress was exposed, the sheets half on, half off. My pillow was torn apart and its stuffing scattered everywhere, like snow. The trophies and knick-knacks usually on my dresser had been knocked down; the bat on my old baseball trophy had snapped in two. My open knapsack lay on the floor, books spewing out. A textbook was splayed open on the floor with chewed-up, soggy corners and shredded pages. The notebook beside it was in similar condition. A laundry basket, once full of my clean, folded clothes, had been flipped onto its side, the clothes pulled into a nest-like pile. Right in the middle of which was Amber, madly rooting and snuffling.

"Amber!" I screeched. She pulled her face out of my

clothes and tiny dark brown eyes looked up at me. Her body twitched with excitement. "No! I don't want to play," I scolded her.

Mom thumped up the stairs. "Did you say 'Amber'?" she yelled.

"Oh, yeah." I stepped aside so she could see into my room. "I found your pig. Look what she did to my room."

"Oh," gasped Mom, as she took in the extent of the damage. "I'll help you clean it up."

"Help me? Why should I have to clean this up at all? It's your pig!" I exclaimed.

Mom frowned. "She's not just mine. She's part of the family. The important thing is, we found her! Poor little thing, she doesn't know any better; this is her way of showing that she loves you."

"By destroying my room?" I asked. "With love like that, I wish she'd hate me."

Mom clucked her tongue and stepped into the chaos that used to be my room. "Bad girl," she scolded and attempted to pick Amber up. That didn't go over well. Amber squealed and squirmed as if being tortured. Finally, Mom gave up and coaxed her out of my room with a chunk of raw potato.

"That's a good girl!" Mom praised when they reached the hallway. She fed her the potato. Good girl? Unbelievable!

I slammed my door shut so hard the frame vibrated.

I thumped about in my room, surveying the damage, before picking up my knapsack with dread. Empty. Oh, crap. I knew what was supposed to be in there. Sure enough, those torn, soggy bits of paper strewn about my floor were all that was left of my geography project notes. I groaned. Anything but that! How was I going to tell Byron the pig ate my homework? I tried to piece the sorry shreds of paper together, but they were too chewed up and slobbery. And there seemed to be a lot missing; most of them must have ended up in Amber's stomach. That pig'll eat anything. I threw it all into the garbage in disgust.

Honestly! The Pig Ate My Homework

Date: Sunday, October 28
Location: The Town Library

"So, who did you say you're meeting at the library?" asked Mom as we pulled out of the driveway and turned onto the road.

"Byron Hopper," I answered.

"And you're working on …?"

"A geography project," I said impatiently. I'd already endured Dad's interrogation back at the house. I hated when he treated me like one of his perpetrators. It was even worse when Mom got into the act.

Mom smiled, ignoring my impatience. "And how is the project going so far?"

I scowled. "Peachy, thanks to Amber." She raised an eyebrow and tightened her lips. We'd said all there was to say about Amber's antics in my room. I sighed and stared out the window.

"So, do you know Byron very well?" Mom was obviously determined to make conversation.

"I know what everybody else knows. Like, his family is in a witness protection program, hiding out from the Mafia. And they're devil worshippers."

Mom made a face. "You're serious?"

I shrugged. "That's what people say."

"What do you think?"

I narrowed my eyes and went for the shock factor. "I hope the stories are true."

"Oh, Sarah," said Mom, with a shake of her head. I smiled. Mission accomplished.

Mom pulled up in front of the library and I stepped out, hauling my knapsack behind me. "Dad will pick you up at four o'clock," she said. "Be nice."

"Yeah. Thanks for the ride," I said and headed into the library.

Byron was already there, sitting at a back table, books out, hood up. He didn't bother to look up when I plunked myself into the seat across from him.

"Hey," I greeted him.

He may have nodded slightly but otherwise ignored me. I needed to teach that boy some social skills! He could at least *pretend* to be happy to see me. I caught him looking as I pulled what was left of my geography textbook and notebook out of my knapsack.

"Got hungry?" he asked with a sneer.

"Oh, uh … funny story," I began, forcing a bright smile. "When I got home yesterday, my mom couldn't find her pig …" He raised his eyebrows and I waved my hand at him. "I know, it sounds weird. We have a pet pig named Amber that lives in our house with us. Anyway, my mom couldn't find her, so we looked everywhere for, literally, hours. Guess where she was?"

He looked bored.

"My bedroom." I made my face look serious as I said my next line. "Byron. The pig ate my homework." Then I laughed. It was a bit forced. Byron didn't join in.

"So?" he asked.

"*So*? Don't you think that's *funny*?" I asked. "A *pig* ate my homework. You know, usually it's a *dog* who eats the homework."

"I know."

I stared at him, exasperated.

"I have a pet iguana," he said. "If I let him, he'd eat my homework, too."

I threw up my hands. "Okay, you win."

"Sounds like you need to be more responsible with your school work so that the pig doesn't get to it," he said.

This guy was too much. I leaned forward in my chair and spoke carefully, as if to a two-year-old, which seemed to be about his level of comprehension. "Didn't you hear me say that it's my *mom's* pig? And that I *found* her in my room? I didn't *put* her there. I don't *keep* her there. I don't even *let* her in there. My room *is* a responsible place to keep my homework."

He shrugged and looked skeptical. It was all I could

do to not shake him. Who did he think he was, anyway? Like he'd never made a mistake in his life — not that I'd made a mistake. No wonder he didn't have any friends.

Byron stood and started packing up his things.

"What are you doing?" I asked.

"Going home," he said, without looking up.

"Why?"

"It's obvious that we're incompatible. It's not really surprising; I knew we wouldn't be able to work together." He zipped up his knapsack and hefted it onto his shoulder. I stood up and yanked it back down. It landed on the chair with a thud.

"You can't just drop me because my mom's pig ate my work. It's not like I fed it to her."

"I'll tell Ms. Lytton we tried but our partnership won't work out. I'm sure she'll understand," he said, hoisting his knapsack back up.

"We're supposed to try for at least a week, not five minutes!"

He stared at me. "How do you know she said that?"

"How do you think?" I was infuriated. How dare he not want to work with me just because of Amber!

Understanding dawned on his face. "Look, if neither of us wants to work with the other person, let's stop arguing about it and just not work together."

We stood silent for a moment. It would have been so easy to walk away from him … but what about learning more about Garnet? And what about my geography mark? He stared at me and swiped at his long brown hair. I stared back. His eyes were big and dark and … sad. I looked away.

"Now who's the one being irresponsible?" I asked quietly. "We were given an assignment and told to work as partners. We don't have to like each other. We just have to get the project done. Besides, maybe we just have to learn to get along. It's a life skill." I couldn't believe I'd just quoted Ms. Lytton.

He didn't say anything at first, then his expression hardened. "Do you know anything about me? I know you're new around here, so have you heard any of the stories?"

For a second, I was speechless, then I decided to be honest. "Yeah, I've heard some stories."

"So why would you want to learn to get along with me?"

"Are the stories true?"

"Maybe." His look was challenging.

"Oh." My mind was racing. Was he admitting to being in the Mafia, being in the witness protection program, or being a devil worshipper? "What do you mean by maybe?"

He shook his head. "It doesn't matter. Like I already told you and Ms. Lytton, I don't work on projects with other people. I like to work alone and" — he turned to leave — "I don't want to learn to get along."

I bit my lip. Here was my way out. I could just watch

him go. He'd talk to Ms. Lytton, I wouldn't have to do a thing. I'd be the rejected victim. I watched his hunched back as he walked away and thought about those sad eyes.

"Byron, wait," I called. "I don't care about the stories."

He stopped.

"Why not?" he asked, without turning around.

"They're just rumours. It's not like you're going to have me thrown into the lake with cement shoes if we get a bad mark, right?"

He turned and gave me a disbelieving stare.

I gulped and forced a grin; that remark was a bit off-side, even for me. "Seriously, I need your help, Byron, I'm stupid in geography. If you can stand me and my irresponsible ways, I'd really like to work with you on this project. Look at it this way: I'm so dumb in geography, you'll feel like you're working alone."

A hint of a smile played on his lips. Either that or he had gas. He strode back to the table, sat down, and zipped open his knapsack. "Okay. Let's work together then," he said gruffly. "But I don't care how stupid you say you are, I expect you to pull your weight. I'm not doing the whole thing myself."

"Fine."

"And for the record, my family's not in the Mafia, okay?" He pulled out his books and notes, laying them out between us while I stared, open-mouthed.

Well, that cleared up one rumour, anyway. For

a brief moment, I considered asking him about the other rumours, then the moment was gone. He started blabbing on about what we had to do and it took all my concentration to follow along. I didn't want him to think I wasn't going to "pull my weight." He might be surly, but he was going to be good for my report card, not to mention my investigation.

At four o'clock we left the library together. There was Dad, sitting in the car, waiting. If he was anything, he was punctual. "C'mere, Byron. I'd better introduce you," I said, tugging on his sleeve. "Oh, by the way, you might want to lose the hood, Dad hates them."

He pulled back his hood, revealing long, shiny brown hair. I stared for a moment; it was the first time I'd seen him without his hood up. Very Bohemian. Dad watched our approach with a smile.

"Hey, Dad," I waved. "This is Byron Hopper, my reluctant geography partner." Dad stepped out of the car and towered over us. Byron wasn't short, but my dad was very tall.

"Nice to meet you, Byron," said Dad, holding out his hand.

Byron shook it and said, "Nice to meet you, too, Mr. Martin."

"*Detective* Martin," corrected Dad. I rolled my eyes. There goes the intimidation factor. What next? Pulling out the handcuffs? Showing off the gun?

"Oh. Nice to meet you, Detective Martin."

"Can I offer you a ride home?"

Byron backed away. "Oh, no thanks. I don't need a ride. I live close by, I can walk."

"I insist."

When my dad insists on anything, it happens. It's just the way the world works. Byron got into the car and told us where he lived. During the entire short drive to his house, the poor guy endured a thorough interrogation. "What do your parents do?", "Do you like sports?", "How are your school marks?" And so on.

It was a bit embarrassing, but thanks to Dad, I ended up learning more about Byron than I would ever have found out on my own. His father was a financial advisor and his mother worked at a local gift shop. He didn't play any team sports but did belong to a karate club, and he played guitar. His grades were all in the nineties.

I was taken by surprise when we pulled into Byron's driveway. He lived in a beautiful home right along the Muskoka River. It was a large brick and wood house with huge windows and immaculate landscaping. It was not at all what I was expecting, given the rumours. I guess I thought it would be more … quiet, small, or … scary.

"Thanks for the ride, Detective Martin," Byron said as he stepped out of the car. "Bye, Sarah."

I waved as we pulled away.

"Nice boy," said Dad.

I snorted. "Nobody's ever accused him of that before. He's usually rude and obnoxious."

"Sometimes people are rude and obnoxious to protect themselves," said Dad.

I frowned. "What do you mean?"

Dad kept his eyes on the road and said, "Sarah, I'm going to tell you something that's not to leave this car."

I sat up straighter, my heart skipping a beat. "Okay. It won't leave this car," I agreed. I couldn't believe it. My dad was going to give me confidential information! I was all ears.

"The police have been called out to the Hoppers' home a couple of times recently —" he began.

"For disturbing the peace?" I asked eagerly. "Animal abuse? Domestic violence?"

Dad glared at me. "And that's exactly why I'm telling you this. Your imagination takes you in the wrong directions. It wasn't for anything like that at all. It was for vandalism. Of *their* house. Seems that someone out there has taken a liking to destroying their property. The Hoppers are the victims."

"Oh."

"So maybe he's rude and obnoxious because that's how people have been treating him," said Dad. "He might be that way to protect himself from getting hurt."

Wow, I had no idea my dad was so insightful.

Disclosure

Date: Tuesday, October 30
Location: School Library

I was on my way to the library after school today to work with Byron when I bumped into my favourite hottie, Chris LeBlanc. He was grinning like a madman and practically bounced down the hall.

"You look happy," I said.

"You bet," he said with a wink. "I'm a happy guy."

We walked together. I'd like to say we made easy conversation, but it was the first time I'd ever been around him when Roy wasn't there too, and I had no idea what to say.

When we reached the library, he asked, "Are you going to the Halloween dance?"

My heart skipped a beat and I nodded, dumbly.

"I'll see you there, then." He gave a little wave and headed down the hall.

I waved back, my heart soaring. Chris wanted to see me at the dance tomorrow night! He must like me! I watched him leave, smiling so hard my cheeks hurt. When he was gone, I turned and walked right into the glass library door, smacking my nose and chin so hard I saw stars. The librarian rushed to my aid, gushing over me, providing a tissue for my bleeding nose. I took the tissue then waved her off, embarrassed, but also incredibly thankful that Chris hadn't witnessed that sorry display. I'm such an idiot!

Byron was sitting at a back table when I approached.

"How far did you get with your research today in class?" he asked.

"Hi, Sarah, how are you? I've been better, Byron, thanks for asking," I answered, still holding the tissue to my nose. I dropped myself into the chair across the table from him. "That's how people have a civilized conversation."

He leaned over the table, his hood falling back from his face, revealing an eye that was puffy and bruised. "Who said I was civilized?" he snarled.

"Right, I forgot," I murmured. I flipped open my books and pulled out the little bit of research I'd managed to complete. "How did you get the bruise under your eye?" I asked.

"How did you get the bloody nose?" he snapped back.

We stared at each other. His face was hostile.

"I'll tell you about my nose if you tell me about your eye," I said.

"I don't really care about your nose."

"I'll tell you anyway." So I did. And he actually

grinned; so he knew how. "You find that funny?" I asked, pretending to be indignant.

"Yeah."

"Thanks a lot," I said, good-naturedly. "Now tell me about your eye."

He glanced at his watch. "We'd better get working; we have lots to do."

"Hey, we had a deal," I protested.

"No, *you* had a deal," he argued. "I didn't agree to anything."

"That's cheap, Byron Hopper … *if* that's your real name."

The effect of my words was immediate. His face darkened. "My family's not in a witness protection program, Sarah," he muttered.

I knew I'd made him angry but I didn't really care. I'd just eliminated another false rumour! At this rate, I'd have this case solved in no time. So, if the Hoppers weren't involved with the Mafia and weren't in a witness protection program, that only left … devil worshipping and murder. I gulped and tried to focus on my notes. I'd rather be working with someone hiding out from thugs than sacrificing neighbourhood pets and stalking neighbours.

A couple of tedious hours later, we left the library together. In the hall, we came upon a tall, lanky boy dressed all in black, viciously kicking lockers. He looked completely out of place in the after-hours quiet of the school. I was at least three steps ahead of Byron before realizing he'd stopped walking.

"What's the matter?" I asked.

"Nothing," he snapped.

"Then, come on."

We continued to walk. The boy stopped kicking lockers to reach into his shirt pocket and pull out a pack of cigarettes. He picked one out and stuck it in his mouth. That's when he saw us. "Byron, my man!" he called around the cigarette, waving his arm.

"You know him?" I whispered.

"Unfortunately," he whispered back. Louder, he called, "What are you doing here, J.D.?"

J.D. was quite a sight. His eyes were outlined in black, and piercings ran all along his eyebrows and in his nose. His black hair stuck up at various angles from the top of his head with longer, greasy pieces falling onto his shoulders. His black T-shirt was torn in various places, revealing a pierced nipple. His tight black jeans were so ripped he might as well have left them at home.

"I'm picking you up, so let's go," he said. "Your sister's waiting out in the car and this place gives me the creeps." He shuddered as if to prove the point.

"I don't want a ride home," said Byron. "I'm walking."

"Too bad. Your mommy told us to get her precious baby boy so he wouldn't be late for din-dins, so say goodbye to the wench and *let's go*!"

J.D. lunged and grabbed a fistful of Byron's T-shirt,

yanking on it so hard that Byron fell forward, arms windmilling wildly.

"Hey!" I shouted, jumping out of the way.

J.D. snorted and made some other awful sounds that might have been laughter. What a creep. I wished my dad was there to put this guy in his place. Unfortunately, Dad wasn't around and J.D. wasn't finished. He yanked the knapsack right off Byron's back and held it out of reach.

"Quit being such a jerk!" yelled Byron.

"Quit being such a girl," scoffed J.D. "What do ya got in here, anyway? Any drugs? I bet mamma's little boy's got some good drugs in here."

"Give it back!" sputtered Byron, snatching at the bag. I wiped my sweating palms on my jeans and wondered if I could get past them down the hall. Before I could make my move, J.D. ripped open Byron's knapsack and dumped everything all over the floor, kicking things right and left. Byron swore and rammed into J.D., knocking him onto his butt.

I braced myself for J.D.'s fury, but to my surprise, as Byron stood over him, fists clenched, he laughed. Like he thought what had just happened was hysterical. I looked at Byron, puzzled. He shook his head in disgust. Once J.D. regained some self-control, he stood up and yawned.

"I'm heading for the car," he announced. "Don't take too long kissing your girlfriend goodbye, little buddy, and don't do anything I wouldn't do." He cuffed Byron on the head before heading down the hall, pausing occasionally for a locker kick.

Byron, his face red and angry, knelt down to pick up his things. I helped him; my hands shook as I handed him his books.

I whispered, "Who was that?"

"That … is my sister's … *boyfriend*," he spat. "J.D., as in Jesse Draker … or Juvenile Delinquent, which suits him better." He wiped his glistening upper lip, then said, "*He's* how I got the black eye."

My eyebrows shot up. "Oh." We walked down the hall towards the exit. "Do your parents know that your sister's boyfriend treats you like that?"

He sighed. "Believe it or not, that was J.D.'s idea of having fun. You heard him, I'm his 'little buddy.' He likes me."

"What does he do to people he doesn't like?" I asked. "What does your sister see in him?"

"He's not the type she used to go for," he said, quietly. "She says she needs him around for her protection."

"Protection? From what?" I asked.

He didn't answer.

We stepped outside where a shiny blue car was waiting, engine running. In the front seat, J.D. was furiously making out with an equally zealous Garnet, the windows fogging up around them.

Byron sighed. "I'd better catch my ride. See ya later." He turned and headed to the car, his back bowed.

I couldn't help it. I felt sorry for him.

I did a little surfing on the net about devil worshipping. Since Byron told me that his family isn't in the Mafia or the witness protection program, I figured devil worshipping was next on the rumour list. What I found out was more than a little spooky.

I really hope this rumour isn't true …

- The term "devil worship" refers to a religious belief in and worship of a devil or devils.
- Devil worship can also be referred to as Diabolatry (from the Greek *diabolos*, "devil," and *latreia*, "worship"), or as theistic Satanism.
- It has been used as a term for those criminals who commit crimes citing the devil as part of their justification.
- Devil worshippers see themselves as the enemies of good and the servants of evil.
- They see the devil as the god of all that is evil. They are reverse Christians.
- Devil worshippers don't believe in magic as being either black or white, it just is magic.
- Rituals are considered an opportunity to manifest justice, for example, if someone wronged you. Devil worshippers don't believe in karma or turning the other cheek.

Creepy. Imagine being a "servant of evil." Ugh!
This doesn't really sound like Byron, I don't think.

Maybe Garnet? She does do that curse thing on people. Would that be a ritual to "manifest justice" on someone who "wronged" you?

Why couldn't they have just been in the Mafia?

The Halloween Dance Disaster

Date: Wednesday, October 31
Location: School, the Halloween Dance

After rolling his eyes at the Sherlock Holmes costume I was wearing to the dance (apparently he thinks there's room for only one detective in our family), my dad agreed to drive Roy and me to the school. As soon as he pulled to a stop, I bolted from the car with a quick "Thanks for the ride!" yelled over my shoulder. Stacey was working at the door, taking money. She was dressed as Catwoman and experienced some difficulty handling the cash around her long claws.

"There's a ton of people here already!" she said excitedly.

"Mindi here yet?" asked Roy.

"Yeah, she just got here."

"What about Chris?" I asked, ignoring the strange look Roy shot me. I'd told Stacey and Mindi about what he'd said to me at the library.

"Chris? Uh ... yeah ... I think I've seen him, too," said Stacey, biting her lip.

"Why do you want to know if Chris is here?" asked Roy.

"No reason," I said, winking at Stacey.

She lowered her eyes. "Uh ... have fun, guys," she said, subdued. She took money from the people behind us. I frowned. What was wrong with her all of a sudden?

We were blasted with loud, pumping music as we stepped into the darkened gym. It looked amazing! Hanging cobwebs draped down from the walls. Black lights shone onto the dance floor, creating an eerie glowing effect on anything white. Stacey was right, there was a good turnout already and the doors had been open for only a short time. My heart lifted with excitement. This was going to be fun!

I scanned the crowd, looking for Chris. Just about everyone wore a costume, making finding a particular person difficult. I should have asked him how he'd be dressed. We finally spotted Mindi by the refreshment table with Cori. I raised my hand to wave but it froze in mid-air. My jaw dropped so far I'm sure it hit the floor. I must have stopped walking because suddenly Roy was ahead of me saying, "Sarah? Are you okay? What's wrong?" His voice seemed to come from far away.

What's wrong? There was Cori, my arch-enemy, snuggled in nice and close to the boy beside her, the boy who stared back at her, completely mesmerized, like he'd died and gone to heaven. That boy was none other than Chris LeBlanc, and he'd never looked at me the way he was looking at Cori. I felt like someone had just slugged me in the gut.

"Sarah?" repeated Roy, stepping closer. "What's the matter? Are you going to puke or something?"

I wanted to crawl under a rug as understanding dawned on me. So that's why he'd said he'd see me here. Because he was going to be with Cori. He'd probably just asked her before running into me. No wonder he was so happy! How could I have been such an idiot? As I stared, I realized that Chris hung onto Cori's every word. Clearly, he worshipped her. Why hadn't I seen it before?

As for Cori, even I had to admit she looked beautiful. How could I blame him for wanting to be with her? She was dressed as Cleopatra and wore a long, shimmering gown with petite golden sandals on her feet. Her eyes were outlined dramatically with black liner, and a gleaming black wig with a golden tiara completed the look. I suddenly hated my dumpy, masculine Sherlock Holmes outfit. What was I thinking? What boy would want anything to do with me dressed like this?

Chris was a dead hockey player. His ghostly white face featured blackened eyes and streaks of blood. His hair was dusted white, and his hockey gear was dirtied and ripped. He looked like he'd just stepped out of the grave. But he still looked good. *Really* good. And he only had eyes for Cori.

I wanted to go home. I might have actually said that aloud to Roy, but by then he'd abandoned me for Mindi. He stood at her side and they laughed at something he'd said. How cute, everyone in couples but me. Would any of them have noticed if I'd turned around right then and left? I took a step back, but Mindi called me over and it was too late to flee.

I was trapped.

Mindi's costume was very cute. She wore a cowboy hat, a silk western shirt, tight jeans, half-chaps, and her paddock boots — all cleaned up so they weren't covered in horse poop. I thought again about my dumpy tweed coat. Why didn't my friends tell me my costume was stupid?

"Ah, isn't that cute?" crooned Cori. "Mindi and Roy are both cowboys! Or should I say, cow*people*."

Yes. Sad but true. Mindi and Roy wore coordinated costumes. He sported a huge Stetson, a red checked shirt unbuttoned practically to his belly (for some strange reason), a pair of my jeans so they'd fit tightly, and full chaps. He even had a coil of rope hanging from his hip, in case he needed to lasso a bull, I guess.

"Well, Cori," explained Roy. "You may think that our costumes are a match, and I don't blame you, but actually, we're not the same at all. You see, Mindi's a cowgirl, just like you thought, but I'm actually an exotic dancer. This is how I look for my most famous act."

With that, he leaned forward and wiggled his eyebrows at her. "You'll see what I mean when I get out there dancing, later on."

She giggled. I gagged.

"Just do us all a favour and keep your clothes on," I said.

"Oh, Sarah!" crooned Cori, snuggling in closer to Chris. "I didn't see you there." Liar. Then she tilted her head and examined me with an exaggerated puzzled expression. "What are you dressed up as, an *old man*?"

My face burned.

"You're Sherlock Holmes, right, Sarah?" said Chris. I nodded, my mouth too dry to speak. "You look great," he added with a smile. Beside him, Cori pouted and tugged at his arm. He immediately turned back to her and she beamed at him.

I sighed. She was such a schmuck and he was such a great guy. Why was he wasting his time with her? Especially when he could be with me! Catwoman, also known as Stacey, joined us just then. She'd finished her shift at the door and had time to enjoy the dance for a while before her next job. I was happy to see her since, like me, she wasn't part of a couple.

"Isn't this the best dance ever? Don't you love all the costumes?" asked Stacey. She grabbed my arm. "C'mon, let's dance!"

I couldn't help but get caught up in her excitement. And I actually started to have a little fun. Roy, of course, had to go a little overboard with the exotic dancer theme. Mr. Sanderson, my basketball coach, ended up giving him a warning about dancing appropriately. When the music slowed down, Chris pulled Cori close. I stared jealously from the sidelines and actually wished I was Cori for just that dance.

Then I saw Byron.

He was staring at me from across the dance floor. I'm surprised I recognized him. He wore a skeleton costume, the bones glowing eerily under the black lights. His face was painted to look like skull bones, his eyes blackened to look hollow. I gave him a little wave just as a couple of dancers blocked our view of each other. When they stepped away, he was gone. I debated for a few minutes before going over to say hi.

I found him heading for the exit. "Byron, you look great!" I said.

"Not great enough. You recognized me," he grunted.

I ignored his surliness. "Why don't you come over and join us?" I asked, while a part of my brain was screaming, *What are you doing?*

He scowled. "No thanks."

"Don't be stupid! Come on over and have some fun," I coaxed.

He looked at me, and suddenly those sad eyes were back. "I just want to head home, Sarah, okay? I only came for a little bit; I never wanted to stay long."

"You put a lot of work into that costume for someone who only wanted to stay for a short time," I said.

"No, my mom put a lot of work into it. Garnet opened her big mouth about the dance, so Mom's giving me twenty bucks to stay for at least twenty minutes," he explained, then checked his watch. "I've done nineteen and a half. Good enough."

"Your mom's actually paying you to be here?" I asked, in disbelief.

"She's trying to get me to go out more," he said, shrugging. "Who am I to turn down easy cash? Besides, I thought I should probably keep an eye on her." I followed his eyes. Off to the side of the dance floor, Garnet was dancing wildly with J.D. "But it looks like she's okay, so I'm heading home."

Impulsively, I grabbed his arm. "Before you go, you're going to come over and hang out with me and my friends."

He tugged back his arm. "No, I don't want to."

But I wasn't taking no for an answer. "C'mon, you'll have fun!"

"Sarah, no. I'm heading out," he insisted.

"Just stay for a little while longer! Maybe your mom will double the money!" I was relentless and yanked on his arm until he finally seemed to stumble along of his own accord. I guess he figured it was better than me making a huge scene by pulling him, kicking and screaming, across the gym floor. I have no idea why I was so insistent. I should have just let the poor guy go home.

"Hey, everyone. This is Byron," I said, approaching the group. Mindi, Roy, Stacey, Cori, and Chris all turned in unison and stared as I rhymed off each of their names. For an extremely awkward moment, no one said anything.

Finally, Chris said, "Cool costume."

"Yeah," grunted Byron, looking down at himself.

"You probably think I'm just a cowboy," said Roy.

"Uh-oh. Not again," said Mindi, grinning.

Roy wiggled his eyebrows at her. "I may look like just an ordinary cowboy, Byron, but in fact, I'm really an exotic dancer."

"Oh really?" I could almost see Byron biting his tongue, holding back a sarcastic response.

"He keeps telling us that if the right song comes on, he'll be out on the dance floor doing his act," said Stacey with a giggle. "We're all trying to figure out what the right song is so we can request it."

"Not all of us," corrected Chris. "I can live without seeing Roy striptease in the middle of a school dance."

"Me too," I agreed. "I saw enough of his butt when we were kids. He used to run around the house naked after a bath."

"Hey, hey, no family secrets," protested Roy, holding up his hands. Everyone laughed. Even Byron — a little.

"So you don't want me to tell them that you still do that?" I asked innocently.

"That's right, it's our little secret."

Byron hanging around with us wasn't as awkward as I thought it was going to be. He didn't say much, just stood beside me. For someone who was known for his obnoxiousness, I thought he did well. That is, until Stacey and I began talking about tattoos.

"I'm going to get one on my ankle," said Stacey. "A flower, I think. That would be cool."

"Are you sure, Stacey?" I asked. "You know you can get an infection from a tattoo needle that hasn't been sterilized properly."

"You sound like my mother!" she protested. "Tattoos are cool! Besides, how many people do you know get infections? I think that's a story parents just made up to stop their kids from getting tattoos."

That's about when Cori joined in. "Sarah, how would you know about tattoos and infections?" she asked. "It's not like you're an expert on the subject, is it?"

I bristled. "I saw a show."

"I think if Stacey wants to get a tattoo, let her get one," said Cori.

"I didn't say she couldn't! I was just saying you can get an infection from the needle," I said. "She should know that."

"She's right," said Byron. We all looked at him, startled. He'd been so quiet, I think we almost forgot he was standing there.

"How would you know?" asked Cori, making a face.

"When I got my tattoo, my mom went with me and made sure everything was sterile and the ink was fresh," he explained. "Then for about a week afterwards, I had to put ointment on it to prevent infection."

Stacey's eyes widened. "You have a tattoo? Can I see it?"

He shrugged and pushed up his skeleton sleeve to reveal his tattooed bicep, which I couldn't help but notice was quite well defined. Looked like he'd be good at arm wrestling. I shook my head to get that image out of my mind. Stacey, Cori, and I leaned in for a closer look. His tattoo was a symbol that looked like a backwards cursive capital *E* with a smaller upside down horseshoe beside it and a script semicircle with a dot above it.

"What is it?" asked Cori with a frown.

"It's Aum. It represents the fundamental sound of the universe," explained Byron.

"The funda ... what?" she asked, screwing up her face. "Where'd you get a weird idea like that?"

"I'm into music and I play the guitar so I thought the symbol for sound was cool," said Byron with a shrug.

"So? I play the piano. That doesn't mean I have to get some weird tattoo on my arm," retorted Cori.

"I like it," said Stacey.

"So do I," I agreed.

"I think it's weird," snorted Cori.

"You don't have to like it," said Byron, pulling down his sleeve. "It doesn't have anything to do with you. It's my body."

"What other weird tattoos do you have? Any other strange symbols?" asked Cori, narrowing her eyes.

"Sure. I'd show you but I'd have to kill you," Byron deadpanned.

Stacey's eyes widened and she backed away.

"He's kidding!" I said. "Right, Byron?"

He looked at me, with that same deadpan expression. "Maybe."

At that, Stacey made a beeline for the refreshment table, mumbling something about checking on the supplies.

"Why would you go and say that?" I asked him. "You've scared Stacey away with your little joke."

"Maybe he wasn't joking," said Cori, who, unfortunately, hadn't bolted with Stacey. "Maybe he's serious."

"Yeah. Maybe I'm serious," echoed Byron.

"Give me a break," I said, exasperated.

Cori shrugged. "Actually, I'm surprised you're here, Byron. Isn't Halloween a big night for people like you?"

"Cori, shut up!" I snapped.

She turned on me. "Why are you sticking up for him? What's going on between you two?"

Before I could answer, Byron said, "I gotta go, Sarah. Cori's right. I've got things to do. It's an important night for people like me." He flipped his middle finger up at Cori as he left. I don't think she saw it, but I did.

"There goes your freaky boyfriend," said Cori.

"He's not my boyfriend." I shook my head and walked after Byron. I'd had enough of Cori and her pigheadedness.

I weaved my way through the crowd and left the gym, looking for him. The hall was deserted except for a couple of teachers chatting and watching the doors. My ears buzzed in the sudden quiet. I felt awful about what had just happened. I shouldn't have forced him to stay at the dance. I should have just let him go home.

A burst of music from the opening gym door announced Mindi's arrival. "Where are you going, Sarah?" she asked. "Did Byron leave?"

"Yeah. Cori ..." I began, then I stopped, unsure what to say. After all, Cori was her friend. I seemed to be the only one who had a problem with her. "I was just going to say goodbye to him."

"Oh." She shifted and looked a little uncomfortable. "Sarah, is there something you're not telling me about Byron?"

"Like what?"

"Well, you seem ... interested in him."

"Interested? Of course I am." Then I caught on to her meaning. "No! Not in that way." I laughed. "You think I asked him over because I *like* him?"

"Well, yeah, I ... we ... were starting to wonder."

"No, it's not like that. It's just ... when you spend time working on a project with someone, you get to know them a little. I guess I'm starting to feel a bit sorry for him. He has no friends. He's lonely. Do you know that his mother paid him to come to the dance?"

"Maybe he's happy that way," said Mindi. "He's not a stray dog for you to take care of."

"I know he's not a stray dog. Look, if he really didn't want to hang out with us, he wouldn't have," I said, trying to forget how he'd fought me when I'd pulled him over to the group.

"Are you sure there isn't something you aren't telling me?" asked Mindi.

I sighed. "Yes, I'm sure. Honestly. I just want to find out the real story behind the Hoppers and clear up the rumours about them once and for all. As for Byron, he's just one piece of the Hopper puzzle to me."

"Okay. Let's go back to the dance," she said.

The music blasted into the hall as Mindi yanked open the gym door. Before following her in, I took a quick glance behind me — and caught Byron standing there, watching. Our eyes met briefly, his full of hurt, before he disappeared around the corner that led to the exit doors.

"Byron!" I called. The gym door closed behind Mindi. I was torn. Should I go back to the dance with Mindi or go after Byron? He'd obviously overheard what I'd just said. I needed to explain myself. Mindi would understand. I hoped.

I jogged down the hall and turned the corner. He

was gone. I peered through the exit door and spotted him, the bones on his costume glowing eerily under the street lights. I hesitated for one brief moment. What did I really know about him and his family? What if he was a devil worshipper? Is that the kind of guy I should be chasing down the street in the dark? Then I stepped outside. The night air was cool and felt good after the hot, stuffy gym.

"Byron! Wait up!" I ran after him.

He didn't respond. In fact, I think he picked up his pace. I called again, a few times. No response. Finally, I slowed to a walk and wondered what the heck I was doing. Should I keep following or go back to the dance? I kept walking while I tried to make up my mind. Next thing I knew, I turned a corner and Byron's massive house loomed in front of me. By then, he was nowhere to be seen. I made up my mind. I wanted to apologize.

I boldly walked up to the front door and knocked. No answer. I realized then that I was just wasting my time; Byron obviously didn't want to talk with me. I turned to leave just as a tall woman with a gorgeous mop of curly red hair opened the door. She was beautiful. My mouth dropped open. If that's what a devil worshipper looked like, where could I sign up?

"I don't have any candy left," she said apologetically.

I looked down at my Sherlock Holmes costume and realized her error. I forced a laugh. "I'm not here to trick-or-treat," I said. "I'm looking for Byron."

"You are?" she asked, looking surprised.

"Yes. He left the dance before I got a chance to talk to him ..." My voice trailed off.

"He hasn't come home yet," she said with a frown.

"He hasn't?"

"No." She stepped aside as if to let me enter and smiled. "Would you like to come in and wait for him?"

"No, thank you."

"Can I tell him who was looking for him?"

"Sarah Martin," I said dully. "We're working on a geography project together."

"Oh! Then I'll be seeing you again," she said with a bright smile. "Do you need a ride anywhere?"

"No thanks, I can walk," I said, stepping down from the porch.

"Are you sure?"

"Oh yeah. It's not problem," I assured her. "I'm not going far."

"Well, okay then, if you're sure. Nice to meet you," she said.

I hit the sidewalk in front of the house and glanced back. Byron's mom still stood in the open doorway. She smiled and waved. I waved back. At that point, I was mad at just about everyone. I was mad at Chris for making me think he liked me. I was mad at Roy for not telling me that Chris liked Cori. I was mad at Cori for being her usual rude self. And finally, I was mad at Byron for not stopping to talk when I called him.

I stomped along the dark, tree-lined sidewalk, getting angrier by the minute, when I heard a noise against the wooden fence between me and Byron's front yard. I spun around. I was alone. Another thump on the fence. This time I saw a stone hit the ground. I still seemed to be alone. A pebble bounced on the sidewalk in front of my feet and I jumped back, heart thumping.

"Who's there?" I called out, my voice trembling.

No answer. No one in sight. My fingers tingled and I made them into fists. Was this some kind of devil curse? Was Byron somehow making pebbles rain down on me? I looked up to the sky to see if any more were heading my way. That's when I saw the eerie skeletal face leering at me from a tree branch on the other side of the fence.

I screamed.

"Oops, did I scare ya?" asked Byron, with a chuckle.

"No, not at all," I answered, trying to steady my voice. I wiped my sweating palms on my pants.

"Liar."

"What are you doing up in a tree?" I asked.

"Hanging out," he said. "What are you doing at my house?"

"Looking for you. I wanted to talk."

"So talk."

"Climb down. I can't talk to you up there," I said.

"I'm not coming down, so I guess we're not talking," he said.

I sighed. Talk about childish. I jogged back along

the sidewalk, through the gate, and back across the yard to the tree. It was massive, with a huge trunk and sturdy branches for climbing. I grabbed one and hauled myself up. Did he think he was the only one who could climb? I'd done my share of gymnastics, so I figured it would be a piece of cake. I soon realized that tree branches were a little different from parallel bars. I managed to reach the limb that he was sitting on and, with a grunt, hefted myself up onto it beside him. Immediately, I lost my balance and felt myself falling backwards.

"Whoa," he said, and reached out to steady me. "Don't climb trees much, huh?" I just glared at him and worked on maintaining balance. "You didn't have to come up here. You weren't invited."

"You invited me when you said you wouldn't come down to talk," I retorted.

"Who said I'd talk to you up here?"

"Me. I just want you to listen anyway," I said.

"I've already heard enough."

"I want you to understand …" I began. I shifted on the branch to get more comfortable; trees weren't exactly lounge chairs.

"I do understand. I'm just a piece of the weird Hopper family puzzle," he said, looking the other way.

I winced. "That's not quite how I meant it."

"There's a better way to mean it?"

"Yes … well …" I hesitated, then decided to tell him the truth. "I had a bit of a run-in with your sister a couple of weeks ago. She sort of tripped over me and then she put a curse on me."

Byron groaned.

"Afterwards, people told me some stories about you and your family. At first, I didn't know what to think. I guess I was a little scared, but mostly, I was curious. Why so many rumours? It didn't seem right. Since we've been working together, you've kindly informed me that you aren't part of the Mafia or in the witness protection program. So, if I can believe you, I know that those two rumours aren't true."

"None of them are true," he mumbled. "We're not devil worshippers either."

I smiled. "That's a relief. But why do all these rumours exist?"

"That's a long story."

"We have time."

"No, we don't. Let's just say, sometimes rumours are easier to deal with than the truth, okay?"

"No, not okay. What's so bad about the truth?" I asked. "What could be worse than people thinking you're a devil worshipper?"

He shook his head. "Sometimes it's just easier to let people believe what they want."

"But ... is it worth not having friends? You must be unhappy ..." My voice trailed off.

"I'm not. What does it matter to you, anyway?"

"Why shouldn't it matter to me? Don't you think

someone should care?"

"No one has up till now." He gazed off towards the road. "Did it ever occur to you that I may not want to have any friends? That if I wanted friends, I'd be a nicer guy?"

"You're a good guy," I said hesitantly.

"I'm not a good guy, Sarah," he said, his expression dark.

"You don't mean that," I said. "Anyway, everybody needs someone to be their friend. You know, to have someone to talk to."

"Like we're talking now?" he asked.

"Yeah."

"I can think of things I'd rather do."

I felt my face go red. I reminded myself that he was probably just being rude to protect himself, like Dad had suggested. "That's your choice; I just came here to apologize. I didn't want you to think the only reason I was being friendly to you at the dance was because I was curious about your family. And I'm sorry if I hurt your feelings." I shifted on the branch, looking for the route down.

"Wait." He was looking at me, a pained smile on his lips. "Thanks, I had fun tonight."

"Until Cori opened her big mouth, right?" I asked.

"Yeah. Until then."

I nodded. "Don't start feeling special, she's not exactly my biggest fan, either."

He grinned. "I gathered that."

"Are you going to tell me why you're sitting in a tree?"

He studied me for a moment. "If I tell you something, will you keep it a secret?"

"Cross my heart and hope to die," I promised, crossing my heart with my hand.

He rolled his eyes. "How old are you?"

"Seriously, I won't tell," I said, dropping my hand.

"Our house has been getting vandalized lately," he explained. "I figure it'll likely happen again tonight given that it's Halloween. I thought if I sat up here, I'd catch the vandals red-handed."

"You're on surveillance!" I breathed. Now that was something I could relate to; I was wearing a Sherlock Holmes costume, wasn't I?

"Yeah, I guess."

"What do you plan to do if you catch someone?" I asked, in awe.

He reached into the neck of his costume and pulled a cellphone out of an inner pocket. "I'll call the police." He looked at my face and laughed. "What did you think I was going to do? Beat them up?" He tilted his head as if considering that option. "Maybe it'll depend on how many there are. I do have a first-degree black belt in karate. I could probably inflict some decent damage, if there are only a couple of them."

"No! You need to phone the police," I insisted.

He laughed again. "I was just kidding. Karate isn't about beating people up," he said. "It's a martial art. It's about self-discipline, controlling your physical energy, and creating inner peace. I'm not training to be a ninja or anything. I like karate because it brings mind and body together."

"Oh. And I always thought it was about beating people up," I said.

"I'm sure I could do that too, if I had to," he added.

I glanced at my watch and tried to make out where the hands were in the dark. "I should probably get going, and this branch is killing my butt."

"I'll walk you back," he said.

"No! You might miss the vandals. I'll be fine by myself," I insisted. I reached around with my foot, searching for the lower branch. I couldn't seem to find it. I reached further and lost my balance. Byron grabbed my arm, steadying me. "Uh, how do I get down?" I asked him.

"I'll help you. Just give me a second." He swung down easily, branches creaking as they took his weight. Then, before I knew it, he was perched beneath me, reaching up.

"Show-off," I said, clenching my teeth.

His hand grabbed my right ankle. I stifled a scream. I couldn't believe how babyish I was being about this. Apparently, I wasn't comfortable climbing down strange trees in the dark. Things you learn.

"I'm going to guide your foot down to the next branch, okay?" he said.

"Sure — not so fast!"

He chuckled. "There's the branch," he said, when he literally placed my foot right onto it.

"Oh, that branch," I said. Okay, I was embarrassed. The branch wasn't that much further down than I'd been reaching.

"Now, lean on it and bring your left foot down," he instructed, his hand still on my ankle. And so it went, all the way down the tree. Byron guiding my foot to the next branch, and I, trembling, letting him. Finally, he held onto my waist as I jumped the remaining distance to the ground.

"Okay now?" he asked. We were standing very close.

"Thanks," I said, sheepishly. "I didn't know I was such a girl."

"Thanks for coming and talking with me," he said.

"You're welcome."

He gazed at me and the moonlight glinted off his deep brown eyes. His hands were still on my waist. Then he leaned down and lightly kissed me. I stood there, stunned, while he climbed back up the tree to watch for his vandals.

"See you tomorrow," I said, weakly.

I jogged to the sidewalk and headed back to school, my lips still warm where Byron's had been. It wasn't until I was halfway back when I realized he hadn't denied the rumour about Garnet's murder investigation. Could that be the truth he was trying to hide from me? That she really was a murderer?

I arrived back at school just in time to see a motley-looking crew made up of Garnet, J.D., a Grim Reaper, a vampire, and a clown standing in the hallway inside the exit doors with Mr. Douglas, the principal, and Constable Meyers, the school's Community Police Officer. As I approached, Constable Meyers wedged the outside doors open. When he turned back to the group, I quickly slipped through them, unnoticed in the commotion.

Mr. Douglas was speaking to the Grim Reaper. "Nathan Tremball, I have to say I'm disappointed in you. I wouldn't have expected this from you."

"I'm sorry, sir. It won't happen again," said Nathan.

"I hope not. You wouldn't want to spoil your good record here," said Mr. Douglas. "But you do understand, after what just happened, that I have to ask you to leave the dance."

"I was only defending myself!"

"Sorry. Rules are rules," said Mr. Douglas, tight-lipped. "As for you, Garnet, this boy" — he pointed at J.D. — "is banned from attending any future dances at this school."

"As if I'd ever want to come back to this dump," scoffed J.D.

"Then I'll be happy not to see you again," said Mr.

Douglas. "You're lucky I'm not pressing charges."

J.D. snorted and swaggered through the open doorway. He was followed by the others. Constable Meyers pulled the doors closed behind them and yanked, ensuring that they were locked. "That'll keep out the riff-raff," he said.

I hurried to the gym, anxious to find out what had happened while I was gone. The gym doors were wide open, displaying a well-lit scene of chaos. The thumping music was muted while kids milled about in groups, talking excitedly. The gym no longer resembled a haunted ballroom. Enough of the decorations had been pulled down and destroyed to ruin the effect. Stacey, Cori, Mindi, and several others from student council were picking up the wreckage and stuffing it into huge garbage bins. Stacey's eyes were red and teary.

Cori saw me first. She pointed accusingly. "Look who's back."

"Sarah! Where did you go?" asked Mindi, dropping what she had in her hands into the garbage.

"Uh, outside …" I said vaguely. "What happened?"

"Some weird guy picked a fight with Nathan Tremball," explained Stacey. "When Constable Meyers told them to leave, the guy went crazy. He wrecked all these decorations on his way out the door. He was with Garnet Hopper. She just watched and laughed."

"And that's why we don't hang out with Hoppers — or their friends," pronounced Cori.

"They ruined the whole dance!" cried Stacey. "And look what that idiot did to all our hard work! Cori's right. The Hoppers are bad news."

"You mean J.D. That's the guy you're talking about. He's the one that's bad news," I said.

"See? Sarah even knows the guy's name. I told you …" said Cori, her voice trailing off.

"Told them what?" I asked, exasperated.

"You're getting really friendly with Byron, Sarah," said Stacey. She had a wary look in her eyes.

"Byron didn't have anything to do with this! He wasn't even here."

"Maybe not, but I bet he would have joined right in if he'd stuck around," said Cori. "He's going to be mad he missed the fun. It's a good thing he left."

"*What?*" I gasped. She was unbelievable! I appealed to Mindi, but she turned away and continued picking up ruined decorations. Then the lights dimmed once again and the music started up. The dance was back on.

I pulled Stacey aside. "You don't really blame Byron for this mess, do you?" I asked her. She shrugged. "Byron hates J.D. He never would have been involved in something like this," I said.

"All I know is that the dance wouldn't have been ruined if he and his freaky sister hadn't come."

"Stacey, that's not fair …"

She left me standing there with my mouth hanging open. Wow. Byron didn't do anything — wasn't even there — and he was somehow to blame for the mess created by J.D. as far as my friends were concerned. Is that what life was like for him? Always getting blamed for things he didn't do?

Roy came up behind me and grabbed my arm. Chris was at his side. "Where have you been?" he asked.

"Aw, were you worried about me?" I asked, sarcastically.

"I'm not kidding around, Sarah. You can't just leave a school dance. Dad would kill you if he found out you were out wandering the streets."

"Are you going to tell on me?" I asked, yanking my arm out of his grip. "Besides, what makes you think I was wandering the streets?"

He lowered his voice. "Sarah, I don't know what's going on with you and Byron, but you need to think about who your friends are going to be."

"Mind your own business," I snapped. I glanced at Chris and felt my face burn. I wished I'd stayed up in the tree with Byron. Why was everyone so against me?

I turned and saw Mindi, Stacey, and Cori with their heads together, deep in conversation. Mindi noticed me watching. She looked uncomfortable and turned away. That clinched it. They were definitely talking about me. Some friends. I walked through the crowded gym, acutely aware of how much fun everyone seemed to be having. Everyone but me. How did the night get so messed up? What exactly did I do so wrong?

The silence in the deserted hallway pounded in my ears. I blindly headed for the exit; I knew when I wasn't wanted. I heard the click of the door behind me and remembered too late that they'd been locked to keep out the "riff-raff." That would be me. A glance at my watch told me there was over an hour to go until the end of the dance. That wasn't so long to wait outside, by myself. No problem.

I walked around the outside of the school towards the front of the building and sat underneath a big oak tree. I pulled my tweed coat tighter around me — it might not be pretty but it was nice and warm — and settled back against the rough bark. I planned to enjoy the peace and quiet. I closed my eyes and proceeded to feel sorry for myself.

It wasn't long before shouting and swearing in the distance interrupted the night's stillness. I sat up. More shouts. Next thing I knew I was on my feet and racing towards the commotion. The noisemakers were the same group I'd just watched get kicked out of the dance. They were squared off in the middle of the road, clearly illuminated by the nearby street light. Garnet stood slightly behind J.D., who was facing Nathan, the Grim Reaper. Nathan's two companions, the clown and the vampire, were at his side.

"Who's your next victim going to be?" yelled Nathan, taking a step closer to Garnet. J.D. moved to block him from her.

"Maybe it'll be you, Nathan!" Garnet screamed.

"Do you think your punk boyfriend is going to protect you?" growled Nathan.

"I don't need anyone to protect me! I take care of myself," Garnet said hotly. In spite of her bold words, she remained standing behind J.D., who was firmly planted, his chest puffed out as if to make his scrawny body look bigger than life.

"Forget about it, Nathan, just leave her alone," said the girl in the clown costume.

"I can't, Leanne, this scum shouldn't be walking our streets," said Nathan, pointing at Garnet and J.D. with disgust.

"So now we're scum?" yelled J.D. He bounced from foot to foot, then suddenly stepped forward and gave Nathan a shove — the same quick movement I'd seen him use on Byron. Nathan recovered, with a little help from his vampire friend, and gave J.D. a push in return. They scuffled for a bit, mostly pushing and shoving.

"Stop it!" screamed Leanne. "Let's just go home!"

Nathan was distracted by her outcry long enough to get sucker-punched in the mouth. He stumbled backward and swung his arm uselessly, in an attempt to strike back. Before any more blows could land, Leanne stepped between the fighters and pushed them apart.

"Stop fighting with this loser!" she shrieked at Nathan. "It isn't solving anything."

"Who are you calling a loser?" yelled Garnet. She

pointed two crooked fingers at Leanne.

Leanne shook her head. "Curse me all you want. It's not like it means anything."

"Oh, it means something," said Garnet, keeping her fingers aimed.

"No, it doesn't," Leanne insisted. "Why don't you get some help, Garnet? You're sick."

Garnet spat at her.

"Gross!" Leanne jumped back to avoid getting splattered. "Maybe you're right, Nate, these people shouldn't be allowed to walk the streets. Let's go." She grabbed Nathan's arm and tugged. The vampire followed.

"Freaks!" called Nathan over his shoulder.

J.D. jumped up and down and punched the air. "Cowards!" he yelled. "See him run?" he asked Garnet with glee, followed by more jumping and air-punching.

"Forget about them," said Garnet, abruptly cutting into J.D.'s little victory dance. "I have to get home."

They headed in my direction, so I jumped the fence of the house beside me and crouched behind a tree. They stalked by silently without even a glance my way. I sighed with relief. Byron had said Garnet thought she needed J.D. around for protection. Maybe she was right. I emerged from my hiding spot and jumped the fence back onto the sidewalk. I jogged after Nathan, Leanne, and the vampire; they hadn't gone far.

"I had him. He got me when I wasn't ready," Nathan

complained. He touched his lip, looking startled as he examined the blood on his fingertips.

"You were in charge, dude," agreed the vampire.

"I'm always in charge, Scott," said Nathan, grinning.

They walked in silence. I followed, careful not to make any giveaway noises. Scott started talking about some concert he and Nathan were planning to go to. Soon, Scott and Leanne turned right and said their goodbyes. Nathan turned left. I followed him. Let's face it, I was locked out of the school dance and had no friends. I had nothing better to do.

I hung back and stayed in the shadows as much as possible, taking care to avoid detection as Nathan made his way down the street. But he'd only gone a couple of blocks when he did an abrupt turnaround and ran straight at me. My heart lurched. Had I been caught? For one awful moment, I froze, not sure what to do. Then I dove onto the nearest lawn, elbow-crawling to take cover behind a tree. I shut my eyes and braced myself for rough hands to haul me to my feet. But, instead, Nathan ran by and turned down the next block. I jumped back to my feet, hot on his trail.

I soon recognized where we were. After all, I'd been on that road once already, earlier that evening. Up ahead, Byron's house loomed. I continued to stay far enough behind Nathan, hiding within the shadows of the trees lining the sidewalk. I searched for Byron's shadowy figure in the big old tree, but he wasn't there.

So much for his surveillance mission. Nathan stopped on the sidewalk across the road from Byron's house and plunked himself onto the ground. I could hear his laboured breathing from where I hid. He sat there for a long time, staring at the house. What was he doing? Was he hoping to pick another fight with Garnet?

After a long while, he stood up and walked across the road. He jumped the Hoppers' fence and jogged along the side of their house. Curious, I crept closer to the fence and peered through. There was Nathan, looking in one of their windows. He was spying on the Hoppers, punching a fist into his open hand, over and over. Next thing I knew, he tore himself away from the window with a roar and snatched something up from the garden, running towards the front porch.

"Ya bunch of freaking witches!" he screamed at the house. He pitched his arm back and winged a pebble at the house. It hit the bricks and fell harmlessly to the ground. Nathan grunted his dissatisfaction and hunted around the garden again. His new ammunition was bigger. This time, he backed up a few steps, closer to the sidewalk.

"Garnet Hopper, go to hell!" he shouted, and the words echoed down the empty street. He heaved the fist-sized rock, grunting with the effort. This time his aim was more effective. The large front window exploded, shattering the stillness of the night. Fragments of glass rained down into the flowerbeds below, the clatter deafening, until only a few stubborn shards clung to the sill, in a stubborn refusal to leave their post.

The window was demolished.

Nathan bolted. He hit the sidewalk and ran past so fast, he was a blur. I stood frozen. In shock. He'd just broken their window. On purpose. The front lights came on. Voices rang through the night, shrill and alarmed. Byron, Garnet, his mother, and a man, who I assumed was Mr. Hopper, appeared at the window, stepping carefully around the broken glass inside. Byron's mother knocked out a few of the dangerous shards and leaned out the window, looking all around. Garnet stood behind her, arms crossed, scowling. I shrank further into the darkness, willing myself to be invisible.

"Who are you?" she yelled, her voice catching. "Why are you doing this?"

The front door crashed open. Byron and his father burst out and ran to the sidewalk, both of them looking wildly up and down the street. Byron looked deranged, he was so angry. I considered stepping out of hiding and telling them what I saw. But how would I explain why I was following Nathan? Would they believe me? Or would they think I threw the rock?

"Come out here and deal with us in person!" his dad bellowed into the night air. My heart beat wildly. That clinched it; I didn't have the guts to step out. Instead, I wished that I'd run, like Nathan.

Byron's mom appeared in the doorway, a phone

against her ear. "Come inside, you two. I'm calling the police."

"Mom, they could still be here," protested Byron. "Dad and I are going to look around."

"No, Byron, your mother's right. This is a job for the police. They'll take care of it," said his dad.

"Yeah, right," snorted Garnet. She wheeled around and disappeared from the window.

"C'mon, son. Let's go inside and leave this for the authorities," said Mr. Hopper, putting a hand on Byron's shoulder. With a final hostile look around, Byron followed his dad back into the house, slamming the door behind him.

I jumped the fence back onto the sidewalk and took off. I wasn't going to be around when the police arrived. I didn't stop running until I was standing safely in front of the school, chest heaving.

Stacey's Good Books

Date: Thursday, November 1
Location: School and Home

Today in geography class, Ms. Lytton gave us time to work with our partners on our projects. I immediately confronted Byron about his lack of enthusiasm for his so-called surveillance mission.

"I thought you were up in that tree to catch a vandal last night," I said, as soon as I sat down beside him.

He looked startled. "I was."

"Where were you when the rock went through your window, then?"

His face was instantly guarded. "What do you know about that?"

"I was there."

"What?" He sat up a little straighter, his hood falling back from his eyes.

"I was there," I repeated. "After I left you in the tree, I got back to the school in time to see J.D. and Nathan Tremball getting kicked out of the dance for fighting.

Garnet and a couple of Nathan's friends left with them. They fought some more outside, then I followed Nathan to your house."

"Nathan? You mean it was Nathan Tremball who broke my window?" he asked.

"Yup. Right after he looked inside."

"He looked in my house? Through which window?" he asked, warily.

"The side one, closest to the fence."

He leaned back in his seat and closed his eyes. "Oh, no."

"What's wrong? What did he see?" I asked.

He opened his eyes, his face unreadable. "Nothing. He didn't see anything."

"He sure thought it was something. That's when he got so mad and called you all a bunch of freaking witches. Then he broke your window."

Byron didn't seem to hear me. "It was Nathan Tremball," he said to himself, softly.

"We have to tell the police. He can't go around vandalizing your house like that."

"We aren't telling anyone." He caught my look of outrage and said, "Sarah, I mean it, do not tell anyone what you saw. If Nathan wants to throw the occasional rock at my house, then I'm not going to stop him."

"*What*? You're the one who wanted to catch the vandal so badly that you were sitting up in a tree!"

"That's before I knew it was Nathan."

"What difference does that make? He has no right —"

"Let it go, Sarah. I'm not turning him in and neither are you."

I bristled at that. Who was he to tell me what to do? "Why were you in the house, anyway? Why weren't you up in the tree watching?" I asked.

He hesitated. "I just had to go inside for a bit, it was no big deal."

"Byron, Nathan saw something in there that upset him enough to throw a rock through your window! What did he see?" I persisted.

He shook his head. "Never mind. It doesn't matter."

"It does matter," I insisted.

"Let it go, Sarah," he snapped. "It's none of your business."

I let it go all right. I stomped back to my desk and worked by myself for the rest of the class. What a jerk. Why was I bothering to be nice to him?

Later, when I was heading to the cafeteria, I met up with Mindi, who gave me the lowdown on Stacey. "She thinks you ruined the dance."

"*I* ruined the dance?" I asked. "How did I manage to do that?"

Mindi sighed. "She said that Byron made her uncomfortable ..."

"What? He didn't do anything."

"I guess he said something about killing people."

"He was joking!"

"Well, it didn't go over too well. And then, that J.D. kid started a fight and ruined all the decorations that she worked so hard on," she said.

"What does that have to do with me?"

"J.D. is Garnet's boyfriend. Garnet is Byron's sister. You brought Byron over to hang out with us," she explained.

I stared at her for a moment. "I'm guilty by association? I still don't get how *I* ruined the dance."

"Well then, you took off with Byron and everyone was trying to find you," she said.

"Wait a minute. I didn't take off with Byron. I took off *after* him to explain what he overheard me saying to you. Then, later, everyone was mad at me because of J.D. I honestly didn't think anyone really cared if I was there or not, so I left," I said, feeling my face grow hot as I relived my embarrassment.

"Well, we did care," she said. "You should have at least let us know you were leaving the school. Roy and I spent the rest of the dance wandering around the gym and halls looking for you."

"I was locked out! Besides, I didn't ask you to look for me," I protested. We arrived at our table in the cafeteria and sat down.

"Where did you go, anyway?" asked Mindi, opening her lunch bag.

I had an inner debate about whether or not I should

tell her about last night's events. She's supposed to be my best friend — actually, she seemed to be my only friend at that particular moment — but part of me wondered whose side she was on. In the end, I made her swear not to tell a soul, not even Roy. And I left out the part about Byron kissing me. I preferred to pretend that didn't happen.

"Wow," she said when I was done. "I can't believe Nathan did that. He doesn't seem the type."

"What type is that?" I asked.

"You know. The vandal type. I didn't think he was like that. He's popular and ... gorgeous! He's on all the school teams."

"He didn't look too gorgeous and team-like dressed as the Grim Reaper and breaking windows," I said dryly. "I told Byron about Nathan this morning."

"What did he say?"

"It was strange; he told me not to tell anyone!"

"Really? That is strange," agreed Mindi.

"The only explanation I can think of is that Byron feels so badly for Nathan because of his brother's accident, and Garnet's involvement, that he would let him do anything he wanted if it happens to make him feel better."

"Sounds like someone with a guilty conscience, don't you think?" she said.

"Guilty for his sister?" I asked. I looked at her, deep in thought. "Byron told me the rumours about his family weren't true."

Mindi frowned. "Of course he's going to say that."

"I believe him."

Mindi opened her mouth to speak but stopped when she saw Cori and Stacey walking into the cafeteria. They waved and headed our way, not looking too thrilled to see me. I spent the rest of the lunch period being totally ignored by them. Everything they said was directed towards Mindi. Cori, I didn't care about, but I really wanted to make things up with Stacey. My chance came after school during warm-ups before our basketball game. We ended up in line together during a drill. I had her trapped.

"Hey, Stacey," I said. She abruptly turned her back on me and glanced towards Cori. "I'm really sorry about taking off during the dance last night and making everyone worry," I said, loud enough for her to hear over the squeaking shoes and bouncing balls. "I didn't mean to ruin anyone's fun, but I got locked out of the school."

"You got locked out of the school?" she asked, turning to look at me, apparently forgetting she was supposed to ignore me.

"Stacey! Heads up!"

The ball was chest-passed to her, interrupting our conversation. She took her turn, dribbled up for a layup, and sank the ball. I took my turn, and missed.

Back in line, Stacey picked up where we left off. "Didn't you leave with Byron?"

"No, he overheard Mindi and me talking about him so I left to explain. And the only reason I got back into the school that time was because J.D. and Nathan were getting kicked out and I sneaked in through the open door."

"So why'd you leave again later?" she asked.

"I … uh … needed to get some fresh air," I stammered.

"Fresh air?" asked Stacey, making a face.

"Uh … yeah. I was really … enjoying the dance … it was the best one I'd ever been to … and I was dancing so much … and getting sweaty … so, I had to get some cool air," I said.

"What about J.D and Garnet? That guy wrecked all my decorations and ruined the haunted ballroom!" She looked close to tears. "And Cori said that they wouldn't have been there if you …"

"I didn't have anything to do with them being there. Don't listen to anything Cori tells you about me. She hates my guts because of her dad, remember?" I said, with a grin.

Stacey smiled weakly. "She doesn't hate your guts, Sarah."

"She doesn't like them."

It was our turns again. This time we both sank our baskets. I caught Cori making a face at Stacey, as if to say, *I told you not to talk to Sarah!* I resisted the urge to stick my tongue out at her.

"So, are we good?" I asked Stacey, when we were back in line together.

She nodded. "Yeah, I guess so. Sorry about today."

I smiled. "It's okay." And it was. I felt like a huge weight was off my shoulders now that Stacey was back to her old self with me. We played a great game and won by a mere two points; the Gryphons were tough. I noticed Roy and Chris in the audience. I wondered if I could ever get Chris to like me more than he likes Cori.

Later, around the dinner table, Dad had some very interesting things to share. We had just sat down. Roy, of course, was already diving into his plate, grunting while he stuffed food into his mouth. I don't know why he bothered with utensils. Sort of reminded me of … Amber. Except Amber's much cuter. I was giving him my premier nasty look, reserved for when he was at his most disgusting, when Dad spoke up.

"There was another report of property damage at your friend Byron's house last night," he said.

"There was?" I asked, feigning ignorance.

"Yes. I followed up on the report today. It happened while you were at the dance last night." He stuffed a huge forkful of spaghetti into his mouth.

"Did you catch who did it?" I asked, trying to sound nonchalant.

"No. I was wondering if one of you heard anything,"

said Dad, around another gigantic mouthful of spaghetti. Gross. So that's where Roy got his table manners. And why hadn't I noticed that before?

"You think it was a kid from school who did it?" I asked.

"We don't have any leads yet. I was just hoping you two may have heard people talking," explained Dad. In went another forkful. That man liked his spaghetti.

Roy decided to put in his two cents' worth. "There was some kid picking fights at the dance. And he pulled down a bunch of decorations before he got kicked out." Funny how much he looked like Dad when he talked with his mouth full.

"Who was that?" asked Dad, putting on his detective face.

I spoke up. "J.D. — Jesse Draker. But Dad, J.D. is Garnet Hopper's boyfriend. Why would he throw rocks at his girlfriend's house?"

"How did you know the vandal threw a rock?" asked Dad.

Oops!

"Uh — Byron told me in school today," I explained, thinking fast. That seemed to satisfy him. "J.D.'s an idiot, but it wouldn't make sense for him to vandalize his girlfriend's house."

"Maybe she dumped him after his little hissy fit at the dance," suggested Roy.

"Now you're making things up. You can't accuse

someone of vandalism when you don't know what you're talking about," I snapped.

"What do you know? You weren't even there when he wrecked the decorations," he snapped back.

"Where were you?" asked Dad, sharply, turning on me as if I just became the lead suspect.

"I ... was in the bathroom," I sputtered. I shot Roy a keep-your-big-mouth-shut look. Luckily he did.

Confrontations

Date: Friday, November 2
Location: School and Byron's House

Nobody else in my family seems to have a problem with impulsivity. Only me. Why is that? Today took the cake. I stewed all through the night because I didn't tell Dad about Nathan Tremball's little vandalism spree, and I continued to worry about it all morning. It was like I was obsessed. That might help explain my behaviour when I saw that red-headed, freckle-faced Neanderthal heading for the gym. I made a beeline for him, without putting my brain into gear first.

"Nathan, wait up!" I called.

He turned, startled to see someone he didn't know calling his name.

"Hi. My name is Sarah Martin. Do you have a minute?" I asked, totally ad libbing because I had no plan.

"Yeah, I guess so. What's up?" he asked, looking puzzled. We walked towards the lockers, out of the main traffic area of the hall.

"I need to talk to you about Halloween night," I said. No sense beating around the bush.

"What about it?" he asked warily.

"I saw what you did at the Hoppers' house."

He took a step away from me, suddenly on his guard. "I don't know what you're talking about."

"Yes, you do. How many times have you vandalized their house, Nathan?"

He threw up his hands and backed away from me as though I had leprosy. "Whoa. Hold on there. I wasn't anywhere near the Hoppers' house Halloween night, or any other night. You got the wrong guy."

"I don't think so. Grim Reaper, right?"

He stared at me, his eyes fierce. I stared right back. To my amazement, his face suddenly crumpled. "I shouldn't have done it," he said, putting his hands up to his face. "I know it was wrong."

"Why did you? What made you so mad when you looked into that window?" I asked.

He dropped his hands. There were no tears, but his eyes looked hollow and empty. He spoke quietly, "I saw them doing some kind of ritual. They're witches and devil worshippers, you know."

"Byron told me they weren't."

"He's lying. His sister put a spell on my brother. And it killed him!" he said fiercely. "*It killed him!*"

"What did you see through the Hoppers' window?" I asked.

He stared off into the distance. "I saw this weird room that had an altar with little statues of people on it. Candles were burning everywhere. The Hoppers were sitting around something on the floor. I couldn't tell what it was. Probably a small animal they were sacrificing or something ..."

I shuddered.

"They were holding hands and chanting strange words. I couldn't make out what they were saying. Something evil." He looked at me, eyes haunted. "They're devil worshippers, I tell you. What they were doing wasn't normal. That's why I threw the rock through their window. To stop them. I think I saved somebody's life. Somebody else's brother. I know it was wrong, but I'd do it again, if I had to." He glared at me, challengingly.

I didn't doubt that Nathan truly believed he'd stopped the Hoppers from doing something harmful. I thought about what Byron had said before he left the dance, about how Halloween was a busy night for people like him. At the time, I thought he was only saying that sarcastically for Cori's sake, but maybe he was telling the truth. He did leave his surveillance post and then refused to explain why. What was so important? A devil worshipping ritual? My stomach grew icy.

Even so, it didn't mean that what Nathan did was right. "Nathan," I said, "you can't just go around vandalizing people's homes because you don't like them.

And what happens if you get caught? Like now? Did you think of that?"

He grabbed my shoulders, his eyes wide in horror. "You're not going to tell anyone, are you? It would ruin my life if people knew about this! My parents would die if I ever got a record. And what would my friends think? My teachers? Promise me you'll keep this a secret. *Please!*" With each word, he was shaking me just a little bit more so that by the end of his plea, I felt like a scrambled egg.

"Nathan! Stop it!" I yelled. He dropped his hands, looking slightly stunned. "I can't promise anything. What you're doing is wrong."

"Please, Sarah," he pleaded. "I'm begging you. I couldn't take it if people knew about this …"

"I have to think!" And with that, I fled the scene.

My afternoon was agony. Drama and science with Cori. All I could think about was Nathan righteously vandalizing the Hoppers' home and Byron lying to me. As soon as science class was over, I headed for the halls, in search of an explanation, but Byron was nowhere to be found. I had exactly five seconds to decide whether I was going home on the bus or not. I decided not. Byron wasn't getting off that easily. A quick call to Dad confirmed that he could pick me up on his way home from work, and I was set.

With every step that took me closer to Byron's house, I got angrier. How dare he lie to me! I stomped up to the front door and punched the doorbell. No answer. I tried it again, holding it down for a couple of seconds. Again, no answer. This just made me angrier. I wanted some answers! I peered through the long, narrow window beside the door to see an immaculate foyer that looked like it came out of one of Mom's magazines. Everything was perfect, from its gleaming tiled floor to the cute little table holding the vase with the careful arrangement of fresh flowers. There wasn't a pair of shoes in sight. Not like at my house where you're constantly tripping over shoes left at the door. Not to mention dirt. According to Mom, we're always tracking it in, so that she can't keep things clean. This floor had no shoes, no dirt, no signs of life.

Except ... I pressed my ear to the door, and sure enough, I heard music thumping and high-pitched laughter from inside. There was somebody home! Why didn't they answer the door? It was then I noticed the blue car Garnet had been driving the other day when she picked Byron up from school in the driveway. I wondered if the doorbell didn't work. I knocked. Nothing. I knocked again, this time like I meant it. I got nothing but sore knuckles. I clenched my teeth; this was extremely annoying. I knew someone was in there and I'd get them to answer the door if it was the last thing I did! I took my fist and hammered. Just let them try to pretend they didn't hear that. I waited for the door to open with my arms tightly crossed. Still nothing. I felt like screaming. You don't get rid of Sarah Martin that easily!

I walked around to the side of the house in hopes of finding another door that maybe someone would actually answer. I had no luck, but I did somehow end up in front of the window Nathan had looked through on Halloween night. The music I'd heard from the front door was much louder there. With a quick glance around to make sure the coast was clear, I dared to take a peek inside.

Garnet was looking right back at me. Startled, I hit the ground and crouched out of sight, my heart hammering. I stayed frozen like that until I realized she wasn't going to throw open the window, stick her head outside, and demand to know why I was spying on her. When my heart settled back into its regular rhythm, my anger returned. If she'd just answered the door when I knocked, I wouldn't have been forced to hide under a window. I stood up enough to cautiously peer over the ledge for a second look. Garnet was exactly where she'd been when I first saw her. On closer inspection, I realized that her eyes were closed. Too bad I didn't notice that before, it would have saved me from near cardiac arrest. She was wearing a long dark robe and held a burning candle in front of her with both hands. She wasn't moving.

She stood in a room that was dark green with bare walls and little furniture, leaving the gleaming hardwood floor almost fully exposed. A couple of armchairs sat in the far corner; a small table holding numerous gourds of assorted shapes and sizes was placed between them. On the other side of the room, a large marble altar was draped with a golden yellow cloth and sported at least a dozen lit candles. Several mini statues of women in robes, or, to be more accurate, in varying degrees of disrobe, were standing amongst the candles, as well as a number of photographs of old-fashioned-looking people. The room was just how Nathan had described it. More and more, it seemed that he was likely right. The Hoppers were devil worshippers!

Garnet began to move. With her eyes still closed, she slowly reached down and placed the candle on the floor. Her newly freed hands made a scooping motion, as if picking up a large object. Then she raised both arms into the air and pulled as if she were grabbing invisible objects down from the sky. Finally, she bent over with her palms facing upwards, gradually straightening and turning slowly in a circle as she did so. With her eyes still closed and wearing a frown of concentration, she continued to move her hands in a deliberate, fluid motion, sweeping them all around her as if smoothing the sides of invisible walls. I suddenly became aware that I'd mashed my face against the window in my eagerness to see, creating fleeting foggy patches on the glass with each hot breath.

"Sarah?" asked a familiar voice.

I screamed and whirled away from the window.

Byron was staring at me, his face puzzled. I had to do some fast thinking.

"Oh, hi, Byron. I was looking for you," I said, trying to keep the tremor out of my voice. I casually stepped onto the lawn as if it were perfectly normal to be standing in someone's garden peeking into their house. "I knocked on the door a few times …"

"So you thought you could just wander around my house and look through my windows," he finished for me. His puzzled look had been replaced by anger.

"Actually, I was looking for another door since no one seemed to hear me knocking at the front one," I explained. "And I could hear music coming from inside so I knew someone was home …"

At this point, I think he'd stopped listening. His face had turned a very unattractive shade of purple. "Did you like what you saw? Did you get your jollies out of spying on the freaky Hopper family? Would you like me to find you a rock to throw?" he yelled. He bent down and grabbed a stone from the garden and shoved it at me. "Here you go! Go ahead. Do your worst!"

"No! It's not like that," I protested, pulling my hands back so that the stone fell harmlessly to the ground between us. "Honestly. I was just here looking for you. We need to talk."

"The geography project is going to have to wait, Sarah," he said. "Things are a little crazy around here since Nath … since the window got broken."

"That's what I need to talk to you about. Nathan and the window," I said.

"I told you already, Sarah. I'm not turning him in; there's nothing to talk about."

"You lied to me."

"Huh?"

"You *are* a devil worshipper. Why didn't you just tell me the truth?" I asked, my voice rising. Anger once again stirring in my chest.

"Shhhh!" He glanced around, as if afraid someone would overhear us. "What are you talking about? I already told you those rumours aren't true!" he whispered.

"Not according to Nathan. He told me a different story today, and based on what I just saw through that window, he's probably telling me more truth than you are," I said.

"What are you talking about?" He stepped into the garden and peered through the window. His face paled in an instant. Stepping back onto the grass, he took me by the elbow and steered me roughly towards the front of the house. "You have to leave now."

"I'm not leaving until I know what the truth is." I planted my feet and crossed my arms.

"I've already told you the truth but you don't want to hear it. You'd rather believe Nathan." He paused. "We don't worship the devil. That's not what Wicca is about."

"Wicca? What's that?" I asked.

He shook his head. "Never mind. You don't really want to know. You'd rather think we're devil worshippers."

"That's not true! I want the truth. Like, did Garnet really kill Nathan's brother?" I asked.

He stared at me wordlessly for a long moment, his eyes furious. Then he turned and headed for the front door. "Leave, Sarah. Go home."

I watched him go. I'd gone too far, I realized. Instead of getting answers from him, I'd slammed the door shut. I looked back at the side window and thought about Garnet and the naked statues. I would have loved to sneak back and see if she was still there, moving her hands all around like a street mime. Was that what devil worshipping looked like? Or did it have something to do with this "Wicca" Byron had mentioned? Lost in thought, I actually took a step back towards the side of the house but stopped when I noticed Byron's pale face staring out from the front window.

Fire!

Date: Saturday, November 3
Location: Mr. Braemarie's Stable

Most days, I find it extremely irritating when Roy barges in on Mindi and me at Mr. Braemarie's stable. But today was different. Because today, not only did he arrive with a hot friend, but also his hot friend was bearing news well worth the interruption.

It was a cool day, and it felt even colder inside the stable. Besides riding Ginger, my favourite horse in the world, I looked forward to filling Mindi in on yesterday's events. I decided to wait until we got out on the trail with the horses. That way, I'd be sure we weren't interrupted or overheard. As I brushed Ginger, I was fascinated by the little puffs of steam that blew out of her nostrils. I discovered I could do the same trick. I was in the middle of showing off our mutual steam-making abilities to Mindi when a distant hooting distracted us.

"Don't owls sleep during the day?" asked Mindi, puzzled.

More hooting, closer this time, followed by an all-too-familiar voice.

"Min-di! Oh, Min-di! Where are you?"

I groaned. "It's Roy," I announced, unnecessarily. Mindi's face beamed. I'm amazed she didn't trip over a pitchfork, she was in such a hurry to get to the stable door.

"Mindi, please don't tell him we're in here," I pleaded.

"We're in the stable, Roy!" she yelled. She stuck two fingers into her mouth and whistled. Very piercing, and not very ladylike. Hadn't this girl ever heard of playing hard to get? She whistled again. I admired her technique. I stuck my fingers into my mouth and blew. I got nothing but spit. I'd have to get her to teach me how to whistle like that. I went back to brushing Ginger, leaving Mindi to visit with Roy without me. I planned to ignore him.

"What's up?" asked Roy as he breezed into the stable. I kept brushing.

"Hey, Mindi. Cool horses. Are you getting ready to ride?" asked a different voice. I froze, the brush mid-stroke. That wasn't Roy. I peeked out from around Ginger's flank. Sure enough, it was Chris.

"Yeah. Sarah and I are getting ready to take the horses out on the trail," Mindi said, giving up my position with a sweep of her hand.

"Hi, Sarah. I didn't see you over there," said Chris. Was it my imagination or did he sound disappointed?

I wouldn't blame him for thinking I was a loser after Wednesday's dance.

Reluctantly, I stepped out from behind Ginger, my plan to ignore Roy suddenly squashed like the still-warm pile of horse manure that I'd accidentally stepped on a couple minutes ago. In fact, I'm sure I still smelled it. I looked down. Yup, there were still bits of it stuck to my shoe. Great. Why didn't I just dab a little behind both ears while I was at it?

"Hi, Chris," I said, with a limp wave.

Roy headed for Thunder's stall. Thunder was Mr. Braemarie's favourite: a feisty black stallion that didn't take guff from anyone. He and Roy had a little routine that Roy seemed to think was hilarious, just because we laughed the first time.

"Hello, horse," said Roy, leaning in to pat his neck. As usual, Thunder kicked the wall and Roy held his hand up. "Whoa! Someone got up on the wrong side of the bed this morning!" Mindi giggled. Why did she encourage him like that? To my surprise, today's routine had a new element. For some reason, Roy reached into the stall a second time and called, "Here, Thunder!" as if he were calling a dog. Thunder, rightly so, was offended. He snorted and nipped the extended fingers. Roy snatched his hand back in alarm, cracking his elbow off the stall door in the process.

"Ow!" he squealed. He attempted to hold both his injured fingers and his sore elbow at the same time. I laughed out loud. Now that was a good routine. Mindi, of course, immediately rushed to his aid and fussed over him, which made it even funnier. I wiped the tears from my eyes and glanced over at Chris. He looked back, grinning right along with me. Maybe he didn't think I was such a loser after all. Gee, compared to Roy, I was pretty cool.

"Can I get you some ice?" asked Mindi.

"Oh, come on!" I said. "He's fine. Quit being such a baby, Roy."

"That wild animal practically bit my hand off!" he yelled, holding up his reddened fingers for me to see.

"There's nothing wrong with you. And that wild animal is a horse. They have flat teeth. Pretty hard to bite off fingers with flat teeth," I said.

"It still hurts," he whined. He turned to Mindi, and his expression softened. "Thanks, Mindi, but apparently, I don't need any ice. I'm just being a baby."

"Are you sure?" she asked, concern in her eyes.

He nodded and gave her a weak smile. "I'm fine. Horse bites don't hurt because they have flat teeth. Funny how doors have flat edges but they still hurt when you slam them on your fingers. But thank you anyway. At least one person around here cares about me."

"Oh, I'm sure Chris cares about you, too," I snapped. "Mindi, let's finish getting these horses ready." At the mention of horses, Mindi tore herself away from Roy and returned to Candy. I resumed brushing Ginger's coat.

"Did you hear about the big commotion at the Hoppers' house last night?" asked Chris.

My ears perked up immediately. "No, what happened?" I asked.

"There were fire trucks and police cars —"

"What?" I exclaimed, alarmed.

"— because they had a fire," he finished.

"Was anyone hurt?" asked Mindi.

"I'm not sure. My mom's friend lives on the same road and she thought that Garnet was taken away in an ambulance," he said.

My hands flew to my mouth. "Is she okay?"

He shrugged. "I don't know."

"How bad was the fire? Is their house burned down?" asked Mindi.

"No. I guess the fire was in one of the rooms on the first floor, and they got it out before it spread," he said.

My mind raced. A room on the first floor … Garnet in an ambulance. I remembered what I'd seen through the window. Garnet, with her eyes closed, a lit candle on the floor and lit candles all over that altar. I swallowed hard and hoped she was okay. I know the girl put a curse on me, but that didn't mean I wanted her to get hurt.

Mindi and I finally did get the horses tacked up, in spite of constant interruptions from Roy and Chris. We trotted them around the fenced field, with Roy mimicking my riding skills the whole time. What a jerk! As if he could do any better. They finally left when we started out on the trail. I'm surprised Mindi didn't invite them to follow us along on foot. I listened absently to Mindi's chatter behind me as the horses took the forest path single file. Since Chris's newsflash, I kept thinking about the fire and Garnet getting taken away by ambulance. What exactly was going on over there at the Hoppers' house? What had Garnet been doing when I saw her through the window?

"Sarah, watch out!" Mindi shouted suddenly. Ginger had walked beneath a low hanging branch. What I should have done was duck; however, since I wasn't paying attention, I didn't. It struck my helmet hard enough to jolt me out of my reverie.

"Ow!" I yelled.

"Are you okay?" asked Mindi.

"I'm fine — guess I should pay attention to where I'm going," I answered, with a grimace. "I can't stop thinking about that fire at the Hoppers. I'm dying to know what caused it."

"I'm sure we'll hear something soon enough," she said.

"I had a very interesting day yesterday," I said.

"Really? What happened?" she asked.

Our horses took full advantage of standing still; they tore up grass with their teeth and chewed noisily as I filled in Mindi. I described my confrontation with Nathan about his rock-throwing escapade and how he begged me not to tell anyone about it. I outlined his description of what he saw through the Hopper's window and how he believed that they really were devil worshippers and that by throwing that rock, he'd interrupted some kind of evil ritual.

She shook her head in disbelief.

"There's more," I continued. "I was mad that Byron might have lied to me, so after school, I went to his house to get the truth out of him once and for all."

"You did? You're either brave or stupid," she said, shaking her head.

"Let's go with brave," I said, with a grin.

"Well? Did you get the truth out of Byron?" asked Mindi.

"No one answered the door when I knocked, but since I could hear music from inside, I went around the side of the house and looked through one of the windows. The same window Nathan was looking into just before he went crazy and threw the rock."

"You looked in one of their windows? That clinches it, you're stupid." She looked stricken.

"Yeah, maybe a bit, but it was worth it."

"Why? What did you see?" she asked.

"I saw Garnet in this weird room that had an altar covered in candles and little statues of women. At first, she was just standing there, then she was moving all around, like this." I moved my arms around in an imitation of Garnet. "I think she must have knocked one of the candles over while she was doing her weird dance-thing. I'll bet that's how the fire started. Something strange is going on at that house."

"No kidding!" She rolled her eyes. "What do you think she was doing?"

I shrugged. "Maybe it was some kind of evil ritual, like Nathan said."

"Wow." She shook her head. "I can't believe you were actually spying on her! You could have been caught!"

"I did get caught … Byron found me there," I said. Mindi's eyes rolled into the back of her head, and for a moment I thought she was going to faint. I put a hand on her arm. "Relax, Mindi. It's fine. What do you think he'd do? Use me as a human sacrifice?"

"*Fine*? How can you say it's fine? He caught you spying on her!"

"I know. And he was pretty mad, but that was nothing compared to when I told him I thought he was lying about being a devil worshipper."

"You *said* that to him? You are definitely certifiable! Why do you do these things, Sarah?" she groaned. "Were you abused as a child?"

In spite of myself, I grinned. "I told you already. I want to get to the bottom of the Hopper rumours."

"Why do you have to know so badly?" Mindi sighed. "Can't you just do your project with Byron and leave them to their lives?"

"No."

"Why not?"

"Because ... I want to know the truth!"

Mindi groaned again.

"Byron did say something to me that might be important. He said something about Wicca," I said.

"Wicca? That's witchcraft. They definitely *are* devil worshippers, then."

I nodded. "Maybe. I want to look into it."

A grunt was her only reply before she pulled her horse away from the grass and nudged it along the trail once again. Ginger and I followed, the Hopper topic closed — for now.

Chris and Roy were playing basketball in our driveway when I wheeled my bike in later that afternoon. Roy was dribbling up to the basket, Chris in hot pursuit. "Who's winning?" I called. Roy swore loudly as Chris swiped the ball right out from under him. "I guess that means Chris?" I asked with a grin.

"Two games to none!" said Chris. "Hey!" Roy had ducked around him while I had his attention, recovered the ball, and put it through the hoop.

"There's no whistle, man," said Roy. "Ya gotta pay attention."

I put my bike in the garage and headed inside. The first thing I did was phone Byron to find out more about the fire. No answer. Then I hunted down Dad, who was in the den watching football. I tried getting information out of him about the latest incident at the Hoppers', but he wasn't sharing anything beyond confirming that there was a fire and that nobody was seriously injured.

I called Byron several more times that evening. No one ever answered the phone. How frustrating!

The Wiccan Life

Date: Sunday, November 4
Location: Home

Byron phoned me back today. Actually, he wasn't technically returning my call so much as cancelling our work session at the library. He told me about the fire at their house and how Garnet got a pretty bad burn on her arm. He was planning to stay home with her and help out with things. Other than that, I couldn't pry any other details from him without risking a hang-up. He sounded too stressed.

A terrible storm blew in over the afternoon. Amber went crazy: squealing, running, and hiding with every thunder clap. By the time the worst of the storm blew over, Mom was exhausted, and I was finally able to sneak off to the computer to find out what I could about Wicca. This is the gist of what I learned:

- The Wiccan Church of Canada was founded in Toronto in 1979.

- Wiccans are pagans. They respect the natural world and worship ancient gods, believing in both male and female gods.
- Their services are called rituals, where they honour the gods and the old ways. They sing, dance, call the gods, celebrate life, burn candles and incense, try to understand themselves and the world, and try to be better people.
- Some Wiccans cast spells and do magic. A spell is like a prayer, a communication, or a request made of the gods.
- Wiccans do not believe in harming others. Many believe in the Law of Three or the Law of Return. In other words, any energy sent out towards others returns to a person threefold. So, if you treat others with love, generosity, and respect, you will receive that back times three.

I also read about circle casting for doing rituals (that's what I now think I saw Garnet doing through the window), creating a sacred space, and calling the elements. Very interesting stuff. Not scary. And definitely not related to devil worship. If this describes the Hoppers' beliefs and lifestyle, I don't know why people are so afraid of them.

Disappearance

Date: Monday, November 5
Location: School and Home

All morning, the school was buzzing about Nathan Tremball. Not because people learned about his rock-throwing fiasco, but because he'd disappeared. The word was that late Sunday night, all his friends had received frantic calls from his parents looking for him. But none of them had seen him or heard from him since Friday night when he was at Jack Simson's party.

After lunch, a school-wide announcement ordered all students to gather in the auditorium for a special assembly. Mindi, Stacey, Cori, and I headed straight there from the cafeteria. To my surprise, Dad stood on the stage with Mr. Douglas, Constable Meyers, and several other teachers. They all had those worry lines on their foreheads and wore that pinch-faced look. Dad's face was grey with exhaustion and his usually pristine uniform was rumpled. He looked like he'd been up all night. Come to think of it, he could have been. He'd been called into work late last night, and I hadn't seen him before heading off to school this morning.

Once all the students had filed in, Dad approached the podium. An expectant hush swept through the crowd; Dad had that effect on people. He stood tall and grasped the sides of the lectern, his eyes slowly scanning the sea of faces in front of him. He cleared his throat. The sound echoed throughout the entire auditorium. Anyone who happened to have been talking stopped immediately.

"I'd like to thank Mr. Douglas, your principal, for allowing me to speak to you this afternoon. My name is Detective Edward Martin and I have a very important request to make." Once again, Dad's eyes swept the room, as if addressing each individual directly. "As some of you may already be aware, a student from this school has been reported missing from his home. Many of you will know him; his name is Nathan Tremball."

The crowd stirred and murmured. Those kids who'd been contacted by Nathan's parents were nodding and whispering to their neighbours. Dad waited for the rustling and murmuring to stop before continuing. "As you can imagine, Nathan's parents are distraught over his disappearance and want nothing more than for him to be found. This is where your assistance is crucial." Dad did yet another sweep of the room with his piercing eyes.

"If any of you out there know anything — or suspect anything — regarding Nathan's whereabouts, you need to come forward and tell us. For Nathan's sake and for his parents'. All you have to do is approach me, or Constable Meyers, or, if you prefer, one of your teachers, after this assembly and tell us what you know. I give you my promise, here and now, that no matter what you say, there will be no one judging or punishing you or Nathan. The only thing we want to do is find him — quickly. So please, if you have any information of his whereabouts, any at all, no matter how sketchy, I'm urging you to come forward." He nodded curtly. "Thank you for your attention."

He stepped away from the microphone. I felt strangely proud of him. Maybe one day, I'd be standing in front of a group of students, making a similar appeal for information. Detective Sarah Martin. Has a nice ring to it.

Mr. Douglas shook Dad's hand before using the microphone to thank us all for our undivided attention. He echoed the urgency of providing the police with information and outlined exactly how we could do that. I guess he figured we were too stupid to get it when my dad told us.

I walked out of the auditorium on autopilot. In spite of the rumours that had been flying around all morning, I couldn't help but feel shocked that Nathan was now, officially, a missing kid. A statistic. I remembered my conversation with him on Friday and how upset he'd become. Could he have been so worried I'd turn him in that he ran away? Or ... did he go back to the

Hoppers' to confront Garnet yet again? Could he have had something to do with the fire that burned Garnet's arm? And then ... did Garnet do something to him? All because I had to go and say something!

What have I done?

Dad arrived home late for dinner, looking exhausted. As we sat together at the kitchen table, I figured it was a good time to ask the burning question on my mind.

"Did you find Nathan?" He looked at me with those tired eyes and shook his head.

"Oh, wow," breathed Roy. "I thought for sure he'd turn up today."

"Let your dad eat, you two. He needs to take his mind off work right now," said Mom sharply.

Dad held up a hand. "That's okay, Gina. I want to talk to them about it."

I sat up straighter. "You want to talk to us about a case? Any time!"

He chuckled. Even Mom smiled. "At least eat your supper first," she said to Dad. "You must be hungry."

She must have been right. I'd never seen a plate clear off so quickly. Not even Roy could keep up. In no time, Dad sat back and patted his full stomach. "That was delicious," he said. A loud burp escaped him.

"Dad!" I scolded.

"Good one!" congratulated Roy.

"Sorry 'bout that. I guess I ate too fast," Dad apologized with a sheepish grin. He winked at Roy. "That was the first chance I've had to eat all day."

"Let's talk about Nathan now," I said, trying not to sound too eager.

"Yes. Let's talk now. Unfortunately, we didn't get any worthwhile leads today after the assembly. I'm surprised. I thought for sure at least one student would've come forward and spilled the beans. It's not too often a kid runs off without telling someone where he's going. Are you sure you two haven't heard anything? What are kids at school saying?"

"All I've heard is that Nathan was at a party Friday night and that he left early," said Roy. "Everyone I've talked to seems shocked to think that Nathan might have run away."

"I saw Nathan's girlfriend in the hall after school today. She looked really upset. I don't think she knows where he is," I said.

"I agree. I talked to her myself today and she seemed quite distressed by his disappearance. According to her, he's never said anything about running away before," said Dad, frowning.

"Maybe he didn't run away," I suggested.

Dad nodded. "That's what I'm starting to think."

How about that? I was thinking like a real detective! I couldn't help but feel a little pride.

Dad said, "So far we've been treating this investigation

as if it were a runaway situation. Typically, a first-time runaway is successfully returned home within forty-eight hours. We're more than halfway there already, and it's extremely important for us to work fast in this case. If Nathan's run off to a bigger city centre, and that's likely what he'd do, he will be an extremely high risk for victimization. He's grown up in a small town and has no experience with street life; it's dangerous out there, and the longer he's subjected to it, the higher the risk.

"But other than a note he left at home on Sunday, falsely stating he was at his girlfriend's house, there's been no sign of him anywhere — that we've been able to uncover, anyway. Not at the train station or at any of the bus pickups. This kid's disappeared into thin air, like magic!"

Goosebumps rose on my arms and a vision of Garnet surrounded by naked statues and candles popped into my head. Nathan seemed pretty convinced that she was a witch and a devil worshipper. Was he right? A sick feeling in my stomach made me put down my fork. What happened after I talked to Nathan on Friday? I know he went to a party, but he left early. Why? Did he just put in an appearance to develop an alibi? Had he already been planning his next visit to harass Garnet?

Dad picked up his glass of milk and downed the whole thing in one swallow, swiping his mouth with the back of his hand. "The more I learn about Nathan, the more I can't help but think that he doesn't fit the profile of a typical runner."

"What's the profile of a typical runner?" I asked, ignoring my heaving stomach.

"Usually kids run to escape an intolerable home situation, maybe involving some kind of abuse or substance use. Statistically, runaways tend to be kids in their early teens and they usually have low self-esteem because they feel neglected and unwanted. They may have emotional or psychological issues. They usually experience difficulties in school and with friends."

"That doesn't describe what I know about Nathan at all," noted Roy.

Dad flung up his hands. "Exactly."

"Do you think he was abducted?" asked Roy, his eyes wide.

Dad shook his head. "There's absolutely no evidence, at this point, to lead us to suspect that. Besides, most often kids are abducted by a parent, but in this case, both parents are present and accounted for. Stranger abductions are very rare, and again, there's no evidence."

"What *do* you think happened?" I asked.

"I'm starting to wonder if there's been some kind of accident. Actually, I'm at a bit of a loss here," said Dad, grimly. "I'm worried that this isn't looking good for Nathan. I need more information."

I knew what I had to do, but that didn't make it any easier. I opened my mouth to speak, but at first, nothing came out. Finally, I swallowed down my nerves and said, "Dad, I think I may have some more information that could help you."

"Oh really? Let's hear it," he said, giving me his full attention.

I took a breath and said a silent goodbye to my previously happy life. Then I told Dad everything. I started with the fight Halloween night and the vandalism (that Byron *told* me about, by the way), and Nathan's reaction when I confronted him about it. I also mentioned how Nathan was convinced that Garnet killed his brother and that she, along with the rest of the Hoppers, was a witch and a devil worshipper.

Dad's expression was thunderous when I finished. This didn't help my unpleasantly churning stomach. "And you're just telling me all this now?" he asked, incredulously. "I stood in front of the entire student body this afternoon, asking for any information, any at all, and my very own daughter is only telling me this *now*? *Seven hours later*?"

Oops. I had a feeling things could get ugly. "I didn't think it was really all that relevant," I explained. Sounded lame, even to my ears.

Dad grabbed the arms of his chair, his knuckles turning white. A remarkable display of self-control, I thought, considering what he probably really wanted to do. "Its relevance is not for you to decide. Is there anything else you're not telling me?" he asked through clenched teeth.

"No, that's everything," I said, biting my lip. "Can I ask a question?" Roy's eyebrows shot up and he did a silent whistle.

Dad closed his eyes and took a deep breath. "I suppose."

"Why did the police investigation of William Tremball's death take so long? Was Garnet really a suspect?" I asked.

He sighed. "You're not to going to leave this alone, are you?"

I shook my head.

"If you must know, there were some things — evidence — that didn't exactly match the story Garnet told the police about how Will's drowning took place. Clearly, it was never enough to warrant charges of any nature. She was cleared. Okay? Satisfied?"

He stood up and grabbed his jacket from the back of his chair. "I'd better get back to work. This kid's on borrowed time — and too much of it's been wasted already." He looked hard at me; I studied my hands, not able to meet his eyes. "If either one of you hears anything else — even if you don't think it's *relevant* — you call me right away. Understood? I won't tolerate any more information being withheld from me. And that goes for you too, Roy!"

Roy and I both assured him we'd tell him anything right away. Satisfied, Dad stormed out the door and was gone.

Dad's Secret Apprentice

Date: Tuesday, November 6
Location: School

Unbelievable! Yesterday, I walked around outside wearing a light jacket and then this morning, I woke up to find everything covered with the white stuff. That's right — snow! Apparently, my family has moved to the Arctic. Roy threw snowballs at me while we waited for the school bus but the snow was too fluffy to stick together and his snowballs disintegrated long before they got to me. This made it easy to ignore him; it's my favourite pastime. It drives him crazy.

By noon, the snow had all melted away. I should know because I was outside doing my part in locating Nathan. I figured that the only way I could make amends to my father was to do everything I could to help with the search for Nathan. My conviction to do just that only strengthened when I got to school. There seemed to be an undercurrent of sorrow everywhere, as if Nathan had died. The school counsellors were working overtime as Nathan's friends tried to come to grips with his mysterious disappearance. Leanne was in the worst state. She walked around like a zombie, looking even more shell-shocked than the day before.

That was why I thought it was so important for me to talk to her. Did she know something about Nathan that could help me piece this Hopper-Tremball puzzle together? Had he told her things and made her swear to secrecy? Things she wouldn't have told my father? When I saw Leanne and a friend heading outside at the beginning of lunch period, I was after them like a shot, splashing melted snow here and there. I quickly caught up to them and didn't waste any time getting down to business.

"Hi, my name is Sarah Martin. My dad, Detective Martin, is running the investigation looking into Nathan's disappearance," I said, all in one breath.

"Did they find him?" asked Leanne, her face lighting up.

"Uh — no. But I'm helping them with the search," I explained. She looked crestfallen. Not such a good start. "Sorry, Leanne, I didn't mean to ..." I cleared my throat. "I have a couple of questions, if you don't mind."

She frowned. "I've already answered all the police officers' questions."

"I have some ... uh ... different ones," I said. "And like I said, I'm helping them. The police are doing all they can — but we need to do more."

"Like what? What more can we do?" asked Leanne, her eyes flooding. "The police told me Nathan probably ran away. If he wanted to be found, he'd just come back, wouldn't he?"

That was when her friend spoke up. "I think you'd better just leave it up to the police to do their job. Leanne's already upset enough about all this." She took Leanne's elbow and stepped around me.

"Thanks, Cathy," mumbled Leanne, allowing herself to be led away.

"Wait a minute! The police don't think he ran away anymore!" I blurted. Both girls stopped in their tracks and turned back.

"They don't? What are you talking about?" asked Cathy.

"Nathan doesn't fit the usual profile of a teenage runaway," I explained.

"What do they think happened then?" asked Leanne.

"Well, other reasons people go missing are abductions, accidents ..." I began.

"The police think Nathan was abducted? You mean kidnapped? Was there a ransom call?" asked Leanne, her eyes wild.

Yikes! Did I say that? "Uh — no! There wasn't a ransom call. They're just keeping all possibilities in mind," I explained, frantically trying to backpedal. "That's why I have some questions to ask you. It won't take long."

Leanne and Cathy looked at each other. Finally,

Leanne sniffed and nodded. I was elated. I'd just gotten permission to conduct an interrogation! I tried to think of a professional-sounding opening question and kicked myself for not being better prepared. Truth was, I didn't really think I'd get this far.

"How long have you and Nathan been going out?" I asked.

Leanne frowned. "The police already asked me that. I thought you had different questions."

Cathy put her hands on her hips. "Are you sure you're working with the police or are you just some sicko trying to get the goods on Nathan so you can spread some rumours?"

"No, I'm not a sicko, and yes, I'm definitely helping the police. Sorry, Leanne, I'll try not to ask you any more duplicate questions, I just thought I'd start with something routine," I said, wishing I had some idea of what questions she'd already been asked — not to mention her answers.

"When was the last time you saw or spoke to Nathan?" I tried.

"Friday night at Jack's party. Cathy and Scott were there, too."

"What was Nathan's mood at the party? Did anything seem odd or out of place?"

"No." She was frowning.

"He left a note for his parents on Sunday indicating that he was at your house; did he tell you about this note before leaving it?" I asked.

"I told you the last time I talked to him was Friday night! No! He didn't tell me about the note," said Leanne, her voice rising. "You aren't working with the police. Those are exactly the questions they already asked me. Let's get out of here, Cathy."

"Wait a minute, Leanne," said Cathy. She turned to me. "Nathan wasn't himself at Jack's party." She glanced at Leanne, who looked away. "He was really quiet and miserable. He hardly spoke to anyone, he wouldn't tell Leanne what was wrong, and then he left early."

"Cathy, he'd been quiet and miserable since his brother's birthday the Saturday before. That has nothing to do with his disappearance," interjected Leanne.

"We don't know that!" argued Cathy.

"Where did he go when he left the party? Did he say?" I asked.

"No. He left because J.D. showed up with some of his goony friends," said Leanne.

"Nathan got kicked out of a dance the other night because of him and he didn't want anything more to do with the guy," added Cathy. "And that idiot, J.D., was saying things to Nathan like 'Garnet is going to take care of you,' as if he was trying to goad him into fighting. Normally, Nathan would have stayed and fought back, but that night, he didn't. He wasn't himself."

I frowned. "What do you think J.D. meant by that? That Garnet was going to take care of him?"

"Who knows," said Leanne, with a shrug. "She must have put one of her stupid curses on him or something. But I thought Nathan was going to freak. His face got all red, the way it does when he's about to lose it, but he didn't. He just said he had to get out of there and he left."

"You didn't leave with him?" I asked Leanne.

She lowered her eyes. "He didn't want me to. But I wish now that I did."

"Did J.D. say anything else about Garnet after Nathan left?" I asked.

"No. He didn't stay very long. He and his friends were crashing the party; Jack kicked them out," said Leanne. Then her face filled with horror. "Do you think Garnet really did do something to Nathan that night and J.D. knew she was going to?"

"No! No, I don't think anything like that," I said. "I'm just trying to gather as much information as I can — for the police." Cathy and Leanne shared glances, both looking skeptical. "Is there anything else you think I should know?"

Leanne shook her head. "Just find him," she said, sniffing. "I don't want anything bad to happen to him."

"The police will find him," I said, hoping I sounded more confident than I felt. They walked away leaving me to my thoughts. More than ever, I was convinced that something must have happened between Garnet and Nathan after that party. She ended up in the hospital with burns and he ended up missing.

Hindsight being twenty-twenty, I should have asked Leanne and Cathy to keep our conversation to themselves. But I didn't. As a result, by the end of the day, the entire school buzzed with rumours that the police suspected foul play and that Garnet was the primary suspect. To make matters worse, I somehow managed to get quoted. I felt like burying my head in a pile of sand — or slush. I had people asking me all sorts of questions. I'd somehow become the expert on the progress of the police investigation.

So much for helping. Could I have messed up any more?

After school, I went to the library to meet Byron for a work session. He was there when I arrived, sitting with his arms crossed and his hood up.

"You want to explain these new rumours about my sister?" he asked, before I'd even had a chance to drop my knapsack. "Seems like you're the go-to person. I guess that explains why you're spying through my windows, doesn't it?" His expression was ugly.

"I can explain …" I began, hating the tremor in my voice.

"That's the only reason I'm here."

"I was asking Leanne and Cathy some questions about Friday night — the last time either one of them had seen Nathan —"

"Why?"

"Pardon?"

He sighed, as though barely containing his temper. "Why are you asking them questions about when they last saw Nathan?"

I cleared my throat. "I'm helping the police."

"Really? Did your dad ask you to do that?" he asked.

"Sort of."

He sat up straighter and leaned towards me. "What's with you?" he asked. "Why do you have to stick your nose where it doesn't belong? Now everybody thinks my sister killed Nathan, just like they think she killed William!" His voice had risen.

"I'm sorry!" I cried. "I didn't mean for that to happen! I didn't say that about Garnet — I don't know why these rumours are going around. I only said that the police weren't thinking it was a straightforward runaway case."

"They don't?" he asked. "What do they think?"

"They're keeping an open mind. Exploring the possibility of foul play or an accident."

"And you told Leanne and Cathy that?"

I hesitated. "Yeah."

He threw his hands in the air. "You see? That's how people jump to conclusions. You provide a little information, discuss an event, they associate the two together, then *bang*! A rumour is born!"

"I didn't mean …" To my alarm, I blinked back tears. "I was only trying to help."

He stared at me. "Are you ... crying?"

"No!"

He leaned closer. "You are."

I turned away and hoisted my knapsack over my shoulder. "I'm sorry I messed things up so much. I didn't mean to — honestly. I'd better go."

"Sarah, wait."

I hesitated and then turned back, wondering what else he could possibly have to say to me.

"Can I trust you?" he asked, with such a pained expression that I felt a pang of sympathy for him.

I nodded.

He examined my face, his eyes so intent I thought they'd burn a hole through me. Finally, he whispered, "I think my sister *is* the reason Nathan Tremball is missing." I sucked in my breath. "Remember what I said to you? About Wicca?" Then his face crumpled. I started. Was he going to cry? Right there in the library? I noted several curious glances our way.

"Why don't we go somewhere more private to talk?" I suggested.

He nodded gratefully.

We headed towards the school's back exit doors as if by silent mutual agreement. I lifted my face to the warm rays of the sun as we stepped outside. After our freakish overnight snowfall, it had turned into a mild, sunny day. We sat on the concrete steps overlooking the track and silently watched the rugby practice in progress. I waited.

Eventually, Byron shifted to face me, sitting so close that our knees almost touched.

"You already know that I don't exactly have a typical family," he said. "But, if you don't want to get mixed up in this, just tell me now and I'll keep it to myself. No hard feelings."

I smiled grimly. "Have we met? I'm already mixed up in this."

"I don't usually talk to anyone about my family ..."

"Maybe it's about time you did. Don't worry, I'll keep it to myself. You can trust me," I assured him.

He gave me a shaky smile and took my hand, staring down at it. "I believe you," he said, then sighed. "The rumours going around about my family are all false. The truth is, we're Wiccan. It isn't something we tell many people because it's so misunderstood. People think that witches ride around on brooms and twitch their noses to cast spells on people. Or worse, they think witchcraft is like devil worship. And it's definitely not like that at all."

"Just like Nathan thinking you're devil worshippers," I said.

"Like Nathan. I made the mistake once of telling him about my family's beliefs and look where that got me. He's the main rumour starter. You see what trusting someone can do?"

I nodded wordlessly, encouraging him to continue. He did after a huge, sad sigh.

"Everything was fine at one time. We practised our beliefs in the privacy of our own home; it wasn't a big deal. That all changed when Garnet was in Grade 8. She and her best friend, Jenni, went a little boy crazy for the high school guys. Garnet had a huge crush on William Tremball, Nathan's older brother. The problem was, he never seemed to notice her, in spite of all the effort she put into making herself noticeable.

"So one day, she decided to cast a love spell to *make* William like her. Well, that's not what we do — cast spells *on* people. Spells are supposed to be like prayers for energy to solve a problem. Wicca law says to harm none. Casting a love spell was more like folk magic, and Garnet wanted to give it a try. So, in spite of everything my parents taught us about right and wrong, and Wicca law, that's what she did. She swore me to secrecy. I didn't really think much of it at the time, I was only eleven, but I do remember thinking that it was only for fun, that it wouldn't really work. But the scary thing was, it did seem to work. Not long after she cast the love spell, William started noticing her and talking to her. Next thing I knew, they were going out and spending a lot of time together. Her friend Jenni was going out with Will's friend, and the two of them bragged to anyone who'd listen about how they were dating high school boys.

"Eventually, our parents noticed how much time Will and Garnet were spending together and they told her that she was too young to get serious about a boy. But when she tried to break it off, he wouldn't listen. Instead, things got worse. He was at our house every day after that, he followed her around at school, and he phoned constantly. It was like he was obsessed with her. It got so bad that Garnet wouldn't answer the phone or leave the house without sending me out to make sure the coast was clear. All she wanted was for William to like her and instead she got a stalker. I think it was because of the Law of Three."

I frowned. "I read about that on the internet. What you do, bad or good, comes back to you, times three. So that if you cast a spell to put power over someone else, which is something you're never supposed to do, it'll come back to you three times worse than you gave out."

He looked surprised. "Right. Basically, if you do bad things, then bad things will happen to you as a result. If you do good, you get good. Karma. Now here's where the story gets really bad. One Saturday in June, it was so hot, Garnet and I were swimming in the river, off our dock. As usual, Will showed up. He was in his parents' boat. They weren't home and he'd decided to go for a little joyride without their permission. Of course, he wanted Garnet to go with him, and he bugged her to until she finally agreed. She was supposed to be watching me while our parents were out so she made me swear to secrecy."

He stopped for a minute and cleared his throat again. His grip on my hand grew tighter. "I waited around and fished off the dock and watched for them to come back. They said they wouldn't be too long; after all, Will had to get back before his parents. It felt like forever, but eventually, I did see the boat returning. They were going way too fast — the river is a no-wake zone, and boats are supposed to travel slowly. Well, they were zipping and leaving wake that rocked every boat along the shore. As they got closer, I saw that Garnet was driving. She pulled alongside our dock like a madwoman, screaming at me to grab the boat and tie it down. She was frantic. I asked her what was wrong and she yelled that there'd been an accident and to go inside and call 911. I was scared so I ran in the house and did just that. Next thing I knew there were police cars, fire trucks, and an ambulance at our house.

"What happened was, they'd boated out onto Lake Muskoka and decided to go for a swim. Unfortunately, the boat's anchor didn't hold and by the time they realized the boat had drifted away from them, it was too late. To make matters worse, the water had gotten really choppy. I found out later there were small craft advisories issued that morning, telling boaters to be aware of rough water conditions." He looked at me miserably. "And I just let them head out onto the lake."

"You couldn't have known that. You were only eleven."

"Right. I was just a kid. I didn't do anything wrong," he said mechanically.

"You *didn't* do anything wrong," I assured him.

He paused and squeezed his eyes shut. I held my

breath and bit my tongue to stop myself from shouting at him to keep going. Then what? What? After a long moment, he said, "Sorry, I didn't think it would be so hard to talk about this ..."

"It's okay, Byron," I encouraged, gently, I hoped.

He continued with a tremor in his voice. "The water was rough and it was a long, tough swim back to the drifting boat. Garnet reached it before William and pulled herself aboard. She's a strong swimmer, but she told me afterwards it took everything she had. There were whitecaps on the lake by then. She threw William a life jacket, but the wind was too strong and it didn't reach him. By then, Will was too tired to fight the waves. She yelled at him to float on his back and rest; she'd get the boat to him. She tried over and over to start it but, in her panic, only ended up flooding the engine. She tried paddling the boat to him using the oar, but that's not easy to do in the best of conditions, and by then the boat was heaving so violently in the choppy water that it was useless. In desperation, she threw him all the life jackets she could find in the boat, but they kept getting caught by the wind and falling short.

"That's when he started to go under. Garnet jumped back into the water, swimming as hard as she could to get a life jacket to him in time." Byron looked into my eyes. "He went down for the last time just before she reached him. She had to dive to pull him to the surface. She gave him mouth-to-mouth in the water, the life jacket holding his head up, but it didn't do any good."

He stopped and swallowed.

"She finally managed to drag his limp body back to the boat and pull him up and in — I have no idea where she got the strength. She gave him CPR until she was so exhausted she couldn't do it anymore. It was about then that she started wailing."

"It's like you were there," I murmured.

He started. "No — we've just talked about it a lot," he explained. "She needed someone to talk to … besides counsellors, that is." I nodded sympathetically. This gave me a new understanding of Garnet. I'd be messed up, too, if I'd lived through an ordeal like that.

"Garnet's never gotten over it," said Byron softly, as if reading my mind. "She'd gotten her Bronze Star just that year and was planning to get her Bronze Medallion and Emergency First Aid certificates, but she's never even been in the water since that day. And the counsellors didn't seem to help — either she wouldn't go to the sessions or she'd just sit there and not talk. The only person she'd open up to was me. Like I knew what to say; I was no help. What it comes down to is she thinks that Will died because of her love spell. She thinks that if she'd never put that spell on him, they'd never have gone out, they'd never have been in that boat, and he'd still be alive today. And no matter what I say, I can't stop my sister from believing that she killed William Tremball. And if that's true, then the Law of Three isn't done yet.

What greater harm is there than to kill another person?" His face was full of pain.

"Is that why the police ran an investigation on Garnet? Because she said she'd killed Will?"

"You know about the police investigation?"

"Only what I heard through the rumour mill and what I read in the old newspaper articles," I said.

He shook his head. "You're unreal."

"Thanks?"

"Yeah, Garnet, in her hysterics, blubbered on to the police about the love spell she put on Will. The police didn't really take that as a confession, although it did cause them to ask more questions than they might have otherwise. And it didn't take long for the Tremballs to catch wind of it. Nathan started picking fights with me; I tried to explain things to him — how we were Wiccan and believed in harming none — but ... that didn't go so well. At Will's funeral, in front of everyone, Mr. Tremball confronted my parents about Garnet and her spell. My parents tried to explain the truth of our beliefs; not an easy thing to do in those circumstances. Needless to say, the Tremballs really didn't understand. It got ugly.

"Mom says it was the grief, that they weren't themselves. Maybe she was right, but after all this time, nothing has really changed. You know, complete strangers used to stop me on the street to accuse me and my family of doing horrible, unspeakable things. And the stories kept growing and spreading so that we were getting blamed for every bad thing that happened in town. You've heard the rumours; even now, they're going strong. We're in the Mafia and running from the law, we're in the witness protection program, we're evil witches, and, my favourite, we're devil worshippers. None of our lives have been the same since that day. The thing about rumours is that once they start, they grow and spread — like weeds. People seem to love gossip." He looked away, his face bitter.

I nodded, remembering how Stacey's and Mindi's eyes had lit up when they told me the stories about Byron's family. We sat in silence for a moment, my hand still clasped in his. I thought about how much I'd wanted to learn the truth about the Hoppers, and now that I'd done it, I felt strangely sad. Sad for them.

"And that's the history of how we got here today. Now, it gets worse," he said.

"Worse? How could it possibly get worse?" I asked.

His face was grim. "Garnet changed after Will's death — a lot. How could she not? No matter what I told her, she was convinced it was her spell that eventually led to his drowning. The extended police investigation didn't help, and neither did Nathan's constant harassment. Think about it: how could she defend herself against him when she believed what he was saying? She started to call herself evil. She lost her love for life; she gave up on her old friends and got more and more goth-like in how she dressed. She got tattoos and tons of piercings. Everything my parents didn't want her to do, she did.

And everything she did seemed to confirm the rumours about us for those looking for some proof.

"My parents tried to be understanding, but what they didn't realize was that Garnet was living in hell. The only reason I'm into karate is because Garnet wanted to learn it to defend herself against Nathan. She dropped out and I stayed in. Then she started hanging out with J.D. He worships the ground she walks on, and she has a bodyguard. A relationship made in heaven, don't you think?" He smiled painfully. "Halloween night, when Nathan looked through our window, he saw us in the middle of a Samhain ritual. That's why he went so crazy."

"What's a Samhain ritual?" I asked.

"Samhain is one of Wicca's four Greater Sabbats. It's a time when we remember and honour those who have died before us and celebrate the afterlife. We believe that our loved ones aren't really dead, but their spirits rest in preparation for their next incarnation. Nathan saw us communicating with our ancestors within the sacred circle, asking them to share their wisdom."

"You were communicating with them? Did they answer you?" I asked, a little creeped out. Byron just looked at me like I was stupid. "Nathan told me you were doing something evil and he threw the rock at your house to stop you from hurting someone. But communicating with your ancestors doesn't sound too evil."

"Like I said, we're misunderstood. Now do you understand why I didn't want you to tell anyone about

Nathan breaking our window?"

"I guess. I still say he doesn't have the right to vandalize your house," I insisted.

He shrugged. "Maybe he does, maybe he doesn't. You know the fire we just had?"

"Nathan did that too, right?"

"No! It was Garnet, casting another spell. A protection spell. That's what she was doing when I caught you peeking through our window." I looked down, sheepish. "When she used fire energy to send her spell, one of the candles fell over. She didn't notice until the cloth over the altar had flames up to the ceiling. She could have burned our house down."

"And Nathan didn't do anything to cause the fire?" I asked, a little disappointed that my theory was wrong.

He shook his head. "Just Garnet."

"So this protection spell she was doing ..."

"Was to keep her from harm. It's because she'd been getting more and more worried about Nathan. She was afraid of him hurting her if he ever found her alone." He caught my expression and quickly explained, "A protection spell is okay as long as it does no harm."

"But ... Byron. Nathan's disappeared!" I cried. "Do you think that's just a coincidence? What if her protection spell did harm?"

He blinked furiously for a minute before saying, "Don't think I haven't thought about that." He lowered his voice to a whisper. "I can't help but worry ... what if

Nathan's dead, too? I mean, I don't think Garnet's spell killed him, but will she think that?" He sagged. "I can't go through a nightmare like that again, and neither can my family or the Tremballs. You have no idea ..." He looked at me, his eyes pleading.

I jumped up from the step. "That's why we've got to do something!"

Byron looked up at me helplessly. "What? What can we do?"

"Nathan's got to be *somewhere*. I don't care if Garnet cast a hundred spells, he can't just disappear into mid-air. It's impossible! We've got to find him!" I paced the pavement, my thoughts racing. "Where are all the places that he likes to go?" I asked. "We've got to conduct a search."

"Aren't the police already doing that?" he asked.

"Well, yeah. But they aren't getting results, are they? So ..." What exactly did I think we could do that the police couldn't? I had no idea, but I couldn't sit around and do nothing! "Byron, what if there's a possibility that Nathan really did run away?"

"What are you talking about?" he asked.

I told him about confronting Nathan about his vandalism and the reaction I'd received. "So, it's possible, don't you think, that maybe Nathan ran away after all? He could have been so worried about me letting the cat out of the bag that he took off."

Byron frowned. "I guess so."

"No matter what happened, we both want to get to the bottom of this and find Nathan. Right?"

He nodded. "Right. But what can we do?"

I thought for a moment. "Something Leanne said keeps bugging me. About how Nathan had been quiet and miserable since Will's birthday two Saturdays ago. She didn't think that it had anything to do with his disappearance, but I'm not so sure."

"How do we find out?" asked Byron.

"We need to retrace his steps over the last couple of weeks. Maybe that will lead us to him."

We decided to start at Will's gravesite. I consulted his obituary, which I'd stashed in my knapsack. October 27 was William's birthday.

"It says William is buried at the United Church Cemetery on Eagle Road," I said. "Do you know where that is?"

"Yeah, just outside of town."

"Can we walk to it?"

"No. But I can get us a ride. C'mon."

We headed to his house, a familiar route to me now. Once there, I called home to explain that I was working late at Byron's on our project and would call when I needed a ride home. Then I followed him to the TV room, where Garnet slouched on the couch with her iPod buds in her ears. One of her forearms appeared thicker under her sweater than the other. The bandaging poked out of her sleeve in a patch of white that moved up and down with her hand as she idly tapped to the beat of the music. I still had questions about how she'd managed to get such a bad burn, but didn't think she'd welcome any, especially from me. I kept my mouth shut.

Byron asked her to drive us out to the cemetery. She glared at him suspiciously while he fed her an excellent story about how we had to do something there for our project. She was reluctant. Finally, he resorted to paying her. That worked.

Then she saw me standing there.

"Do I know you from someplace?" she asked, her eyes narrowed.

I shrugged and tried to look innocent. "Maybe you've seen me around school?"

She shook her head. "Whatever."

I couldn't believe my luck: she didn't remember the tripping incident! It was like Mindi had said: give it time and she'd forget all about it. What a smart girl.

As Garnet drove, she snapped her gum and drummed on the steering wheel, paying minimal attention to the road. Her black hair was pulled up into high pigtails, so from where I sat I had a clear view of her right ear. I counted the piercings. I got to nine when she caught me.

"What's your geeky little friend looking at, Byron?" she asked.

"I don't know, Garnet, why don't you ask her?" he said.

"What are you looking at, kid?" she asked me with a sideways glance.

"I like your earrings," I answered, with what I hoped was a winning smile.

"Right." She scowled.

Before too long, she turned into the cemetery. By that time, the sun was low and the street lights had come on. Garnet drove through the open gate, and a sea of tombstones faced us. Actually, it was more like a pond. It wasn't a very big graveyard, dwarfed by the surrounding forest. We were the only car in the parking lot.

"Did you know that people are just dying to get in here?" I asked, feigning seriousness. Byron chuckled. Garnet looked bored. More snapping of the gum.

"How long are you going to be? My favourite show's on in twenty minutes," she complained, glancing at her huge black watch.

I jumped out of the car. "We won't be long. C'mon, Byron."

I walked among the tombstones, reading them as I passed. Soon, we found the one we were looking for. Byron read the inscription aloud: "William Jonathan Tremball. Beloved son of Nancy and Gregory Tremball. Brother of Nathan Tremball."

I got misty, and I blinked furiously to clear my eyes. I'm not sure why, there wasn't anything unusual or unexpected in what he'd read. It just seemed so ... solemn. To think that William's body lay under the ground right here in this spot. It was sad. And a little creepy. I think I'll go for cremation.

"Look, fresh flowers." I pointed to the bouquet that was resting at the foot of the headstone. "They must visit regularly. It's so sad, isn't it? That they had to celebrate his birthday here," I said, staring down at the grave.

"Yeah." His face was in shadow, but I think I may have seen something glistening.

"What are you two *doing*?" shrieked Garnet. I whirled around, startled. She was standing right behind us. I hadn't heard her approach. She stepped closer to the tablet. "Why are you looking at Will's grave?" Her face was furious. "I thought you were doing something for school?"

"We are. We just found it, that's all," said Byron. I had to hand it to him, he could think quickly in a pinch.

Unfortunately, Garnet wasn't buying it. "You did not. Byron, what's going on?" she asked, her hands clenched by her sides.

"It was my idea," I blurted.

"Yours?" she shrieked again. "What do you know about Will?"

"I know that Nathan was upset after Will's birthday two Saturdays ago, that he's been targeting you over the past couple of weeks, and that now he's disappeared," I said, surprising myself, not for the first time, with how good I am at speaking before thinking.

Garnet totally flipped. "Byron! What's going on here! Who is this little freak? You said you needed to come here for your school project, and now she's trying to frame me for Nathan's disappearance?" She pointed at me with two fingers and hissed. I assumed I was getting cursed again. And she called me a freak!

"No one's trying to frame you, Garnet," said Byron in a quiet voice. "We're trying to help."

"Help? How?" she cried.

"We're trying to figure out what happened to Nathan," he explained.

"We know what happened to Nathan. I happened," she whispered. "Again. I killed both of them. Two brothers."

"No, Garnet! You didn't," insisted Byron. "You didn't make William drown, I —"

"And we know Nathan's been doing a lot of things he's not proud of lately," I interrupted. "I think he just ran away. You haven't killed anyone."

"That's what you think, but you don't really know. You don't really know anything," she said darkly.

"Garnet, stop," said Byron.

It was then I discovered the picture. I repositioned the flowers that had tipped onto their sides and there it was. Lying underneath. I picked it up. It was a framed photo, sealed up in a plastic sandwich bag. Two boys, one a younger Nathan, the other (I recognized from the obituary) William. They were sitting together on a huge rock, a towering birch tree behind them, water lapping at their feet. Both of them were holding fishing poles and grinning widely.

"What do you have there, Sarah?" asked Byron.

"It's a picture of William and Nathan," I said.

"Let me see that!" ordered Garnet. She snatched the photo out of my hands and examined it. "I remember this day. I took this picture from the canoe."

"You did?"

She nodded, her eyes glistening. "I went with them — once — to their favourite place, a tiny island on Lake Muskoka. They used to go there all the time, just the two of them, to hang out, talk, and fish. Nathan was mad when Will brought me along that day, he kept saying it was their secret place and no one else should be allowed there."

"Do you mind if I take it to show my dad?" I asked. "I think it might mean something."

"Why would your dad want to see it?" asked Garnet.

"He's running the investigation that's looking for Nathan," said Byron.

"So you really are trying to find him?" she asked.

I nodded.

I was barely home ten minutes when Mindi called.

"What's going on between you and Byron?" she asked, without even saying hello.

"What do you mean?"

"Cori saw you two sitting together on the back steps at school today. She said you were holding hands and so into each other that you didn't even notice her. What's going on? You told me you were just doing a project."

"We are. He was telling me —" I began.

"Sarah, Stacey and I warned you about him."

"I know, but —"

"Cori said you looked like you've totally fallen for him. Have you? Why were you holding hands?" she drilled.

"We were —"

"Cori warned me that there was something going on between you two after you dragged him over to hang out with us at the dance. But you said there wasn't and I believed you. Now this! You can't get involved with him, don't you understand?"

"Mindi, I —"

"What do you think people are going to say if they see you hanging all over Byron Hopper? Cori says it'll ruin your reputation. We already told you that everybody hates him. Do you want people to hate you, too? What are you trying to prove? Well?"

She finally stopped talking long enough for me to respond. Apparently, Garnet wasn't the only one who tried to manipulate people, and Cori didn't need to cast any spells.

"Mindi, calm down. There's nothing going on

between Byron and me. We were just talking, that's all," I said, irritated at having to explain myself.

"Why were you holding hands, then?" she asked, practically shrieking.

"We were practising one of our tasks for the independent project. It's a role play," I lied. I hated to do it, but hopefully it was just a temporary measure. I'd explain everything to her later, in person, when she was calmed down.

"A role play?" she asked, sounding immensely relieved. "You two aren't having a thing?"

"No," I insisted.

"Oh, what a relief! I'd better phone Cori right now and tell her that before she spreads it all over the school." She hung up.

I sat for a while staring at the phone, stunned once again at how easily rumours started. I didn't like the feeling of being judged based on hearsay.

Byron must feel like that all the time.

Dad finally came home around nine o'clock. I raced down the stairs to greet him.

"Hey, Dad! Did you find Nathan?" I asked.

He scowled. "No. There's no trace of him anywhere. It's like he's disappeared. I've never seen anything like it." He rubbed his head as if it ached, then rested a hand on my shoulder. "And how was your day? Hear anything more at school?"

"Actually, I did. I have some things to tell you," I said proudly.

"Good. Follow me," he ordered. "I need all the help I can get on this one."

We headed for the kitchen. I just about tripped over my own feet in my eagerness — Dad really wanted my help! I impatiently watched him heat up the dinner Mom had set aside for him, wanting his full attention when I gave him my report.

"Well?" he asked, as he finally settled at the table, warmed dinner in front of him.

"I had a long talk with Byron Hopper today and he gave me some background information about his family and the Tremballs that you should hear," I reported, feeling important. Then I proceeded to tell him everything that Byron had told me about Garnet's spell casting, William's drowning, and Nathan's growing hatred for Garnet. I explained how we'd visited William's gravesite, and I showed him the picture I'd found leaning against his tombstone.

"You mean to tell me you took this photo from the boy's grave?" asked Dad, not looking quite as happy and excited as I'd anticipated.

I hesitated for a moment. "Yes."

"Did it not occur to you that you were stealing?" he asked, his face reddening.

Oh, boy. I bit back my retort stating the obvious: the guy's dead, what did he care if we borrowed his photo?

Instead, I said, "I thought it could be a clue. You said to tell you anything we learn — anything at all — to help you find Nathan. That's all I'm doing. I just wanted you to see it; I'll put it back."

He seemed to calm down a little, so I guess I said the right thing. Somewhat reluctantly, he took the picture from me and examined it while I explained what Garnet had said about it being the brothers' favourite place. My hunch was that perhaps Nathan had gone there.

"To do what?" he asked, setting the photo onto the kitchen table.

"I don't know. Escape? He was pretty upset when I confronted him about the Hoppers' window. He was terrified that I'd tell and tried to make me promise not to. And who knows what else he's done? The guy was on the edge, Dad."

He looked skeptical. "Thank you for telling me what you've learned, Sarah, but I'm not sure how any of it is going to help me find Nathan." He gave me a funny look. "Do you believe all this witchcraft stuff, like spell casting and the rule of three thing?"

"The Law of Three," I corrected him. "And no, I don't believe that Garnet's spells really did anything, but she believes they did and that can be just as dangerous, don't you think? I just thought you should know that there's bad history between these two families. Maybe there's something to the fact that Nathan disappeared shortly after Garnet cast her protection spell, or maybe there isn't. Maybe it's because I confronted him about his vandalism. But you said it yourself, this isn't a typical runaway scenario. Something happened to make Nathan disappear. I think we should find out what it is."

"And what do you suggest I do with your information — you know — to help me find Nathan?" asked Dad. I swear his mouth twitched, like he was trying not to laugh at me.

I tried to ignore it. "Maybe you should talk to more of Nathan's friends. Or find that island. Or show me your case notes … " I said, my voice trailing off as he grew more incredulous by the moment.

"All his friends have already been interrogated, Sarah," said Dad. "We can't go turning this into a witch hunt." Then, realizing his pun, he raised his eyebrows and chuckled. "Get it? A witch hunt?"

"Dad, I'm being serious!"

He held up a hand in apology. "You're right, sorry. As for going to the island … do you have any idea where it is? And he'd need a boat to get there, wouldn't he?"

I nodded miserably.

"His parents have not reported their boat missing. For that matter, no one in Muskoka has recently reported a stolen boat. I doubt that the boy would swim to the island, even if it wasn't November."

"But …"

He held up a hand. "As for my case notes, you know I can't show you them. You're not an OPP detective."

183

"Well, not yet. You can consider me your apprentice," I suggested. Seemed reasonable to me. Unfortunately, he didn't agree. He laughed. I bristled.

"Sarah, when I asked for help, I just meant information. I only wanted you to keep your ears open at school. I didn't really mean that I needed you to work for me," he explained.

"You mean I'm supposed to tell you everything I find out but you're not going to tell me anything or let me do anything," I countered. He got that look on his face. The one that meant I was pushing him too far.

"Yes, that's right. This isn't a contest, Sarah. We need to find that kid. And you will continue to tell me anything you hear that may be important in finding him, like you just did. But the information flow goes one way and one way only. To me!"

I wanted to argue back, but I knew when I was talking to a brick wall where Dad was concerned.

"I told Byron and Garnet you would help," I said, trying not to pout.

"I am helping. I'm leading the investigation into Nathan's disappearance. I'll find him, Sarah. And when I do, Garnet will realize that her spells are harmless fun. There's a real explanation for his disappearance. Okay? So, keep those ears open — that's how you can really help." He tweaked my ear and gave me a wink.

How condescending.

I whirled and stomped out of the room.

I couldn't stop thinking about Nathan. Was he out there on that island? Or was he in some kind of an accident, like Dad had mentioned? Or did Garnet actually do something to him with her protection spell? I felt helpless just sitting around, doing nothing. I kept thinking about that photo. Obviously, Nathan thought enough of it to put it at Will's grave. It meant something — I just knew it!

I called Byron.

"We have to do something," I said as soon as he answered.

"Most people say hello first when somebody answers the phone," he said.

"You're giving *me* a social skills lesson now? That's a laugh," I said. "Seriously, we've got to do something. And I mean yesterday."

"I take it your dad didn't think much of the photo."

"Never mind him. He's doing what he needs to do, and we're going to do what we need to do," I said.

"Which is …?"

"We have to find that island from the picture." I guess I was as surprised as Byron when those words came out of my mouth, but as soon as I said them, I knew that's what needed to happen.

"Why? You can't honestly think Nathan's been … living … out there for the last two days? He isn't crazy! It's November. Do you know how cold it gets at night?

We had snow the other morning! And how do you think he got there — swam? Don't you think his parents would know if their boat was missing?"

Jeesh! Sounded like he'd been speaking with my dad! "I didn't say we'd find Nathan there — although that would be nice — I just think we might find something that will lead us to him. Some kind of a clue. I don't know. I just have this feeling that it's important and we need to go there."

On the other end of the line, there was silence.

"Do you have any better ideas?" I challenged him.

And because he didn't, and because he was desperate enough to go along with anything, we came up with a plan.

Waterlogged

Date: Wednesday, November 7
Location: Lake Muskoka

I dressed in layers when I got up this morning since Byron warned me that it would be chilly on the lake. Actually, I think what he said was that I'd better not whine about being cold out there because it was all my idea. In the kitchen, I packed tons of food, in case there was nothing else to do but eat during my wild goose chase. I'd just thrown in a last-minute bag of chips and was searching through the fridge for pop when Roy joined me.

"Hey, what's Amber trying to get in your bag?" he asked.

Sure enough, Amber was having a great old time snuffling her way into my open knapsack, her pudgy legs pedalling against the floor for leverage as fast as they could go.

"Amber! Stop it!" I tried to pull on her snout, but it was no easy task. When that pig makes up her mind to do something, it's difficult to change it. I tried a new tactic and heaved on her fat little body.

"Get out of there, Amber," I grunted. She was strong. Behind me, Roy howled with laughter. Finally, she pulled her snout out of my knapsack. Voluntarily. Not because of anything I did. Three Twinkies and a licorice stick hung out of her mouth, half devoured. She happily mowed the rest of them down, wrappers and all. I took advantage of her preoccupation and zipped my knapsack closed. Safe from the beast!

"Wow! Are you on some kind of new eat-like-a-pig diet? What else do you have in there?" asked Roy, reaching for my bag.

I put it behind my back. "Don't make me wrestle you, too."

"Like you'd stand a chance." He frowned. "Hey, what's with all the sweaters?" he asked, pulling at the neck of my top layer.

I slapped his hand away. "Pervert! None of your business." I hoisted up my laden knapsack with a grunt and tried to step around him. He blocked my way. I stepped in the other direction. He blocked me again. Talk about aggravating! Then, before I could defend myself, he grabbed the knapsack off my shoulder and unzipped it. He kept it out of my reach as he looked inside, giving a low whistle.

"Look at all the stuff in here! Going on a picnic?" he asked.

"No — a field trip. So I need extra food and clothes."

"I don't remember you saying anything yesterday about going on a field trip," he said, eyes narrowed.

"Like I tell you everything. Jeesh! You're so suspicious!" He tried staring me down, but I stood my ground. "Okay, you've had your fun, now let me by." He didn't move. "*Mom!*" I yelled.

"Leave her alone, Roy," called Mom robotically, from upstairs. I gave him my sweetest smile, and he stepped aside.

"You're up to something," he said, staring at me.

"Whatever!"

I made it to the front door without any further challenges from Nosy Roy and got my jacket out of the closet. I was in the middle of stuffing my oversized arms into the sleeves when Amber decided to launch another attack on my knapsack.

"Oh, no you don't!" I cried, kicking the bag away with my foot while I finished dealing with my jacket. Inside, the bag of chips crunched. "No more Twinkies for you, little girl," I said when she waddled closer, snout working furiously. I leaned down and scratched her back. She could be a pain sometimes, but she sure was cute. "Wish me luck, Amber, I'm going island hunting. Don't tell anyone," I whispered.

Then I shouted goodbye to Mom and ran out to catch the bus, with her yelling, "*Have a good day!*" behind me.

I sure hoped so.

I'd only been in homeroom for approximately thirty seconds when I ran for the washroom and pretended to throw up, Mindi hot on my heels. She then went back to report that I was sick and going home, unknowingly providing me with a cover story for my absence.

As I was making my escape from school, I ran into — of all people — Cori.

"Where are you going in such a rush?" she asked, not bothering to hide her contempt since we were the only two people in the hall.

"Home. I'm sick," I said, barely slowing down.

"You don't look sick," she said.

"Well, I am!" With that, I put my head down and burst out of the doors into the cold morning air.

First Amber, then Roy, and finally Cori. Why couldn't they all just mind their own business? By that time, I felt like I really could throw up. I'd never skipped school before in my life. It was totally nerve-wracking! Lying to everyone, making up cover stories — I didn't like it one bit! I was definitely cut out to be on the good side of the law.

All the way to Byron's, I kept glancing behind me, scared that at any moment Mr. Douglas would be chasing me down the road. I had to remind myself that I'd volunteered to do this — in fact, it was my idea — so I had to stop being such a wimp about it. On the bright side, I arrived at Byron's house right on schedule. He had the front door open before I even had a chance to knock and pulled me inside.

"We're ready to go," he said.

"We?" I asked, startled.

He cleared his throat. "Garnet's coming with us."

"What? That's not what we planned," I protested.

"I know. But she overheard me talking to you on the phone last night and figured out what we were doing. Either she comes with us or she's calling our parents and ratting us out."

"You've got to be kidding."

"She'll do it, too," he said. "It'll be fine. We could use her help finding the island. She's the only one of us who's actually been there."

I had to admit, that did make sense. However, when I came up with this hare-brained idea, spending the morning in a boat on Lake Muskoka with an alleged murderer wasn't part of the plan.

"Fine, then. Let's just get going," I snapped.

He looked me up and down. "You're going to need this," he said, pulling an enormous, bright yellow slicker out of the closet.

I held up my hands. "I'm not wearing that."

He gave me an exasperated look. "I'll take it anyway, in case you change your mind."

"Fat chance," I mumbled under my breath. I followed him through the house to the back door. Their yard was long and ended at the Muskoka River, which, according to Byron, led into Lake Muskoka. Garnet was waiting on the dock watching our approach. She waved. Beside her, in the water, was an old, battered tin boat with a tiny, rusty motor. I blinked. Try as I might, I couldn't even see a steering wheel. That couldn't be what we were using. I thought these people were rich! Where was their big boat?

Byron saw the surprise on my face. "We do have another boat, but it's been winterized so we can't use it."

"Winterized?"

"The fluids drained from the motor, covered, stored ..." He saw my blank face and stopped. "Never mind. This is the boat we have for today. It'll be fine. I use it all the time for fishing and boating up and down the river."

So much for a luxurious cruise in fine comfort! Byron and Garnet stepped aboard and waited for me to do likewise. I seriously considered walking back to school at this point. Then Byron held out a hand and steadied me as I took a tentative step in. The boat immediately wobbled under my weight, and I fell down hard on the seat. Yup! This was going to be fun.

Byron sat behind Garnet and me, in the *stern* (so I was informed), where he could operate the outboard motor and the steering — without a steering wheel, as suspected! After about half an hour of Byron tugging on the starter rope, which had an uncanny resemblance to the one on our old lawn mower at home, he managed to get the crusty old motor to start. Holding my nose against the overpowering smell of gasoline, I wondered again what I'd gotten myself into.

"Is this thing safe?" I asked.

Byron chuckled. Did he not know I was serious? "She's never let me down yet!" he yelled over the deafening motor.

We didn't exactly choose the nicest day to spend on the water. There'd been frost on the ground that morning and the air was more than a little chilly. A spooky mist curled up from the river, sidling along the sides of the boat. I imagined we were in the middle of a horror movie, and at any moment a veiny, blood-soaked claw would reach up from the murky depths below and drag me down to my everlasting doom. I slid further towards the middle of the boat, just to be safe, even if it did bring me closer to Garnet.

Sitting in "Old Tin Tippy," as Byron and Garnet affectionately called their unsafe little raft, we were perilously close to the water. In fact, there seemed to be as much water trying to get into the boat as there was underneath us. Once we got to Lake Muskoka and were able to pick up speed, it got even worse. Waves sprayed into the boat and onto my legs. I glared jealously at Garnet, sitting beside me in her yellow slicker, staying nice and dry. If I didn't do something soon, I'd be completely drenched in icy water. I snatched up the big, ugly yellow slicker that Byron had brought for me and looked back in time to catch his smirk. Forget pride, I wasn't about to get pneumonia.

As we motored along, at what felt like breakneck speeds, the icy wind and spray numbed my face. It was too loud to have a decent conversation, thanks to the sleek condition of the motor, so I had plenty of time to think. Yet again, I found myself doubting the wisdom of this decision. I tried to remind myself how certain I was that the photo was an important clue, not to be ignored. And how finding the island in the picture could lead us closer to Nathan. But all I kept thinking about was how much trouble I was going to be in when my parents found out what I'd done. Let's see, we'd skipped school, stolen a boat — well, sort of, it did belong to the Hopper *family* — and tampered with a police investigation. At least, that's how Dad would see it. Finally, Byron cut the engine and we slowed down. I took advantage of the relative quiet to speak.

"We've been out here for hours; are you sure you know where this island is, Garnet?" I asked, my teeth chattering despite three sweaters, a jacket, and an ugly, bright yellow raincoat.

Garnet glanced at her watch. "It's only been about twenty minutes, Sarah," she said. Oh great. When twenty minutes feels like hours, you know you're in trouble. "And yeah, I know where the island is. Keep going and stay to the left, Byron, it shouldn't be too much further now. We can't miss it — look for the big birch tree and the rock by the water's edge."

He revved up the engine once again, making conversation impossible, and followed her directions. We passed several small islands, but each time, Garnet shook her head and motioned for Byron to keep going. I squinted my eyes against the cutting wind and noted that Byron seemed to like driving very fast. I hoped the frail little boat wouldn't fall apart at those speeds.

After what felt like an eternity, Byron slowed and cut the engine. "Garnet, it couldn't be this far out. Are you sure you know where this island is?"

She hesitated. "Yeah. It shouldn't be too much further. You need to keep going."

"That's what you said over an hour ago," he said.

"Well … I remember it taking us a long time to get there," she said.

"Yeah, you were in a canoe. I think we've missed it." He started up the engine again and turned the little boat around.

"What are we doing?" I yelled over the engine's rattle.

"We're going to keep looking for the island — but this time, I'm not listening to Garnet!" he shouted.

"How do you know where you are?" I asked. After all, there were no street signs.

"Don't worry, Sarah," said Garnet, putting her hand on my shoulder. "We've been boating on this lake since we were kids. Byron knows it like the back of his hand."

"And how often does he look at the back of his hand?" I asked. I didn't want to be argumentative, but really! How often does anyone really look at the back of their hand? I sure hope he knew the lake better than that!

Garnet just chuckled. "You're crazy."

Byron guided the boat all around every island we happened upon, looking for the telltale birch tree behind the huge rock at the water's edge. But none of the islands we found looked just like the photo. After a while, I was so numb with the cold, I stopped shivering. I wondered if that was a bad sign.

Finally, Byron killed the engine. "Why don't we eat something?"

I glanced at my watch. I was startled; it was almost noon. We had planned to be back at Byron's house by then so that we'd only have to skip our morning classes. My stomach won out over my anxiety about skipping school, however, and I eagerly pulled out the food I'd brought — minus the Twinkies and licorice that Amber ate, of course. Between the three of us, we had quite a feast.

"So, are we heading back now?" I asked once our bellies were full, stuffing the leftovers back into my knapsack.

"I think we should stay out here and keep looking," said Garnet.

"Sarah and I only planned to spend the morning," said Byron.

"I don't think we should give up so easily, do you?" asked Garnet. "We're out here now, we might as well keep on looking. What if we're almost there? If we turn around now, we'll miss it. Do you want to take that chance?"

She made a good point. "She's right," I agreed. "We've come this far."

"We'll keep going, then," said Byron.

Part of me wished he'd put up more of an argument. In spite of my earlier certainty that we had to find the island from the photo, I wanted to head back. Noon? It felt more like midnight. My butt was absolutely numb from the hard seat. I longed to stand up and stretch, but since that would most likely result in me toppling into icy water, it wasn't going to happen.

The afternoon went much like the morning. We circled every island we found, looking for the birch tree and the rock from the photo. The lake seemed to go on forever; I couldn't believe how many islands there were. What had I been thinking? Sure, let's go out and find the Tremballs' island, no problem. And to make matters worse, the day seemed to get colder as time went on. Every once in a while, the sun would peek out from behind the clouds and warm my face a tiny bit, but overall, it was windy, freezing, and miserable. The waves continually slapped the sides of the boat, and their spray kept our beautiful yellow slickers permanently wet. By mid-afternoon, with still no sign of the boys' island, I finally caved.

"I'm ready to go home," I announced. "This hunch isn't working out the way I'd hoped."

"No!" cried Garnet.

I turned to her and said, "Garnet, Nathan's going to be okay. His disappearance has nothing to do with you or your spell. I thought finding his island would give us some clues, but ... it's not going to happen."

She didn't answer. Byron shook his head sadly and turned the boat around for our journey home. We had travelled a fair distance — I was in the middle of mentally promising myself that if I didn't get caught skipping this time, I'd never do it again — when Byron cut the motor and pulled a rolled-up, laminated map out of his knapsack.

"What are you doing? Are we lost?" asked Garnet, looking startled.

"We're not lost," he snapped. "I know where we are — generally. I'm just not sure I recognize this shore line so I thought I'd check ..."

"C'mon, Byron, you never get lost out here. Not even when you drove the boat back after Will's accident. And you were only eleven years old then!" said Garnet with a wave of her hand. Her mouth suddenly dropped open, her eyes wide. "I mean, when you and I were ..." Her voice trailed off, and she looked away.

I froze. Behind me, I felt Byron's eyes bore into my back. Garnet's words echoed in my head. *He didn't even get lost driving the boat back the day of Will's accident.* He was there! But he'd told me that Garnet and Will were alone on that boat and he was left at home. Why would he lie about that?

"Sarah ..." said Byron behind me. I shut my eyes and didn't answer. What was I doing with these people I hardly knew? People that no one else would ever choose to be around? "Sarah, I can explain ..." said Byron.

All this time, I'd believed the things he'd told me, and yet he was lying about the biggest thing of all. "Why didn't you tell me you were on the boat with Garnet and Will the day he died?" I asked.

"I couldn't tell you because we didn't tell anyone. Not even the police," he said. "And that wasn't my idea. It was Garnet's."

"I was just trying to protect you!" she cried.

"I didn't need you to!" yelled Byron. "I've been living with this guilt for the past two and a half years! I would have been better off with everyone knowing the truth right from the beginning!"

My whole body grew numb. "What's the truth, Byron?" I asked, partially scared to hear it, but needing to anyway.

"Byron, no ..." warned Garnet.

He ignored her and stared at me. "I'm the one who killed William Tremball," he said at last. He lowered his eyes and turned away from me.

"You are not, Byron! Don't say that! It was an accident!" cried Garnet.

I felt like I'd been punched in the stomach. I couldn't believe what I'd just heard. "You killed William?" I asked.

He nodded and looked miserable. "It wasn't on purpose."

I scrambled to the bow of the boat to get as far away from him as possible. In my haste, the boat rocked dangerously. I tumbled sideways, and my arm plunged up to my elbow into the icy water. The shock took my breath away. I regained my balance and grabbed the sides of the boat, holding on tightly as it steadied.

"You almost tipped us over!" yelled Byron.

"She didn't mean to, Byron. She's scared," said Garnet.

"No, I'm not," I said stubbornly, shaking my drenched arm.

"And you shouldn't be. I'm not a serial killer. It was an accident!" he shouted.

"Stop yelling at her!" cried Garnet.

"I want to go back," I said.

"Sarah, please listen to me. I can explain," he said, lowering his voice.

"Let's just go back now," I insisted.

He stared at me, his jaw clenched. Then he consulted his map. Soon the motor started and we were speeding through the water. I still sat in the bow, facing him. There was no way I was taking my eyes off him now. My mind raced. No wonder the evidence at the accident scene didn't match Garnet's story — she was covering up for her brother! I kicked myself, yet again, for believing Byron's lies and putting myself into this dangerous situation: trapped in a recklessly unsafe boat with a self-confessed killer! Someone who'd killed another human being — while *on a boat!* I felt panic building in my stomach. I briefly considered jumping overboard to escape, but the thought of my whole body becoming as frozen as my sopping arm was a major deterrent.

The boat gave a sudden lurch, interrupting my troubled thoughts.

"What was that?" I shrieked.

"Uh-oh," said Byron quietly.

Panic fluttered in my stomach. "Uh-oh? What do you mean, uh-oh?"

Another lurch. Then another. After a series of sputtering noises from the engine, we floated silently on the water.

"We've run out of gas," said Byron.

"You've got to be kidding!" I screeched. That was the last straw. That's when I knew I'd never survive the day. Why didn't I listen to Mindi and Stacey and leave the Hoppers alone?

"Did you bring the extra gas can?" asked Garnet.

"No."

"What? Mr. Organized didn't bring extra gas?" exclaimed Garnet.

"The tank was full when we left. I thought we were

just going to be out for the morning," explained Byron. "You're the ones who wanted to stay out longer. How was I supposed to know we'd have to travel the whole lake to look for the stupid island?"

So now it was a stupid island. Was everything Byron said about wanting to help find Nathan a lie too? I grew numb with my next thought. Did *he* do something to Nathan? To protect his sister the way she'd protected him all these years? He seemed awfully worried about her. And, thanks to me, he knew about Nathan vandalizing his house. Did he take matters into his own hands and …

"What are we going to do?" asked Garnet.

"Calm down, we'll be fine," said Byron. "We need to get over to that smoke. That's where I was headed anyway, hoping that someone could point me in the right direction. Maybe someone there will have some gas we can borrow to get back."

"Hey! I have my cell with me. I can call for help," said Garnet.

A wave of relief splashed over me. "You can call my dad," I said. "He'll get us some help."

She pulled it out of her knapsack and stared at it. "Oh. No service."

"Great!" I threw my hands up, the panic back. "Now what are we going to do?"

"Relax, Sarah," said Byron. I stared at him. He tells me he killed someone, we run out of gas, and he says to relax? Was he for real?

Byron partially stood up. Once again the boat rocked dangerously, making me cling onto the sides. He reached down and pulled out two paddles from under the seats and fit them into the oar locks. He sat back down, facing backwards, and began to row. We were mobile again, heading towards the rising, curling line of smoke in the distance. I closed my eyes and formulated an escape plan.

It took him a while, but Byron finally beat the battle against the waves and got us to the island where the smoke was coming from. Rocks jutted out of the water, like teeth, barring us from entry to the shoreline. The closer we got to the rocks, the rougher the waves, tossing us so violently I thought for sure we'd be dumped. We hit the first rock with a bang that just about jarred me right out of my seat. We then scraped and bumped every rock in our path. I held on for dear life, and the Tin Tippy got a few more dents to add to its already impressive collection. Icy water sprayed high with each wave that hit, and since I was sitting in the bow, I was getting the worst of it. In spite of the ugly slicker, I was soaked through, and my teeth chattered so hard I thought they'd shatter in my mouth.

Finally, Byron found an opening among the rocks closest to shore. He wedged the boat between them, and it swayed and scraped within its stone prison, bumping us into land. That was my cue! Before either of them could stop me, I hopped out of the front of the boat and scrambled over the rocks, stumbling and soaking my legs up to my thighs. Once safely on shore, I hightailed it towards the smoke. I ran like I'd never run before. I had to get away from the crazy killer siblings — I had to get to safety.

"*Sarah, wait!*" yelled Garnet after me.

I ignored her. Behind me, I heard Garnet swearing loudly. I picked up the pace, keeping my eyes on the thin spiral of smoke in the distance; there was no way I was going to be their next victim. That smoke meant a person, a person who was going to save my life. Byron and Garnet kept calling for me to stop as they crashed through the bush after me. I ran faster. Soon, the smoke was directly ahead through the trees. I burst into the clearing that was the source of the dying fire and stifled a scream.

A body lay motionless, curled up in a fetal position next to the waning flames. I rushed forward and dropped to my knees beside it. "Are you okay?" I asked, reaching out to shake a shoulder.

Just then, Byron stumbled into the clearing, gasping for breath. "Why did you run from us? What's wrong with you?"

"It's Nathan!" I yelled, momentarily forgetting that Byron was the enemy. "We found Nathan!"

He stopped, his anger replaced by shock. "Is he alive?" he asked softly.

"I'm alive," came a weak voice. I jumped.

"Nathan!" cried Byron, rushing forward, dropping to his knees beside me. "You're okay!"

Nathan struggled to sit up; his arms trembled with the effort. "I'm starving."

"We have food," I offered, as I helped him to a sitting position. "In my knapsack ... that I left in the boat."

"I'll go back and get it," offered Garnet, who had silently joined us. She took off at a run.

He smiled gratefully, then his smile vanished as recognition dawned. "*Sarah*? What are you doing here?"

"I'm helping the police find you," I said.

"Are you turning me in for what I did?" he asked, his face horrified.

"No! I just wanted to find you," I assured him.

"And I'm helping her," added Byron.

Nathan stared at us, then visibly relaxed. "In that case, I guess I'm happy to see you," he said, with a smile. "Are the police on their way, then?"

"Uh ... sort of," I mumbled vaguely. How could I tell him that we'd arrived, lost, in a boat with no gas?

"How did you find me?" asked Nathan.

"It's a long story. This is going to sound crazy, but we were out here looking for the island you and Will used to go to all the time. We found the photo you left at the cemetery."

"You did? Why ... " At that point, Garnet arrived back with the knapsacks. At the sight of her, Nathan's eyes widened. "You!"

"Garnet came with us. We were all trying to find you, Nathan," said Byron.

Nathan stared at each of us and shook his head. "I'm confused. Why would Garnet try to find me? We hate each other."

"I don't hate you, Nathan," said Garnet quietly.

"Here, why don't you eat something and then we'll explain," said Byron. He gave Nathan a bottle of water and one of the remaining sandwiches I'd packed that morning. He snatched them up, drinking and eating greedily.

While he ate, I grabbed a few of the sticks and branches that he had piled up and threw them onto the fire. They caught instantly, the flames rising higher. I stood close, grateful for the heat. By then, Nathan had polished off a second sandwich and was looking a little less grey.

Garnet started the conversation, picking up where they left off. "Nathan, I know you hate me now, but we used to be friends a long time ago, remember? When I was going out with your brother. Don't get me wrong, I don't blame you for hating me … " Her voice trailed off.

"No! It's time to stop the blaming and the hating," interrupted Byron. "Both of you. What happened to Will was an accident. A horrible, horrible accident! And it wasn't even Garnet's fault!"

"Okay, wait a minute! What are you saying? That Garnet didn't mean to put a spell on my brother, and that she didn't seduce him onto the boat that day, letting him drown while she watched?" he said, tears springing to his eyes.

Garnet winced.

"Stop it, Nathan!" yelled Byron. "Enough!" He cleared his throat. "Look, I'm going to tell you some things and you're going to listen. I'm tired of Garnet and my family being bad-mouthed by people who don't have all the information. And I'm tired of people vandalizing my house and me not doing anything about it."

Nathan glared at me.

"Hey, I didn't promise I wouldn't tell," I said.

He turned back to Byron, his eyes hard. "Go on."

"Nathan, my family is Wiccan. We are not devil worshippers, like you've spread all over Muskoka. We aren't running from the Mafia or living in a witness protection program, either. We believe in living in peace and respecting other people. We don't believe in casting spells to manipulate people. Our law is to harm none."

Nathan snorted.

"I'm not saying we're perfect, but that's how we try to live. We're only people, and we can only take so much. Thanks to Will's accident — and you — our lives have been a living hell, testing us in our beliefs like we'd never imagined possible."

"You think your life's been a living hell?" challenged Nathan.

Byron nodded. "I know it's been that way for you, too. That's why you need to know the truth of what happened that day on the boat."

"Go on," said Nathan, his voice steely.

"Garnet did everything she could to save Will. It was me — if I hadn't have been there ..."

"If you hadn't have been there, Will and I would both be dead," said Garnet hotly.

"Wait a minute, what are you saying? You were on the boat too, Byron?" asked Nathan, surprised.

Byron nodded. "I was on the boat too."

"But ... I thought ..." said Nathan, frowning.

"Garnet told the police she was the only one there to protect me. I wish she hadn't, but I was only a kid and I was scared to death. So I let her. Biggest mistake of my life," said Byron.

"What really happened?" I asked.

"Our parents weren't home, and Garnet was watching me. So when Will showed up on his parents' boat, wanting Garnet to go out on the lake with him, she didn't have much choice but to drag me along. Believe me, it was the last place I wanted to be. We boated for a while; I mostly sat in the stern and sulked. When Garnet and Will decided to go for a swim, I was so bored that I lay down across the bow of the boat and dozed off. Next thing I knew, Garnet and Will were yelling and calling my name. I woke up to see them still swimming, really far away. The boat was rocking like crazy because the wind had picked up so much. We didn't know that a storm was blowing in; it was like it came out of nowhere.

"By then, Garnet and Will were waving their arms and yelling at me to start the boat and get it closer to them. I tried. I honestly did. I couldn't get it to start. The whole time, they were screaming at me to hurry, and I was trying, but I couldn't get the stupid boat to start." His chin trembled. We waited for him to continue. "Garnet got to the boat first. She could hardly get her breath she was so exhausted, but she climbed aboard and shoved me out of the way. She got the motor started, no problem. I felt so stupid that I hadn't been able to do it myself. She turned the boat around and headed towards Will. By then he was really struggling against the waves and starting to panic. You could see it in his face. When we got closer, I threw him a life jacket, but the wind carried it away so that it was too far for him to reach. Garnet threw another one at him but the same thing happened — the wind was too strong. By then, Will was really tired." Byron hesitated, eyes moist. "That's when he went under for the first time."

Beside me, Garnet sobbed. I blinked back my own tears.

"Garnet jumped into the water to help Will. He was going under and couldn't get to the life jackets we'd thrown him on his own. She was trying to take him one, but she got too close. In his panic, he grabbed her and held on, pulling her down with him. He was so strong, she couldn't get loose. I yelled for him to stop, to let her help him to the boat, but he was beyond listening.

He kept struggling and fighting and he was so strong. I had to do something or they were both going to drown. By then, all three life jackets were in the water, I had nothing else to toss them. I saw the paddles and picked one of them up, thinking I could reach out with it and they could grab hold. They were right there, not far from the boat.

"I leaned over the side and held out the paddle, yelling at Will to grab it. But he wouldn't listen. Or maybe he couldn't. By then, Garnet was barely getting a breath; Will kept pushing her under to get himself above water. I ... I kept reaching out with the paddle and yelling at him to grab it and hold on. He could have just grabbed it. If he'd only just grabbed it. We were so close to getting him aboard. If he'd just stopped fighting us, we would've done it ..." His voice trailed off. Garnet kept crying. "You have to understand, Nathan, I thought they were both going to drown right there, in front of me. In his panic, Will was drowning my sister. I had to do something. Please understand. I had to do *something*." He gave Nathan a pleading look.

"What did you do?" asked Nathan, his voice breaking.

Byron looked away. "I ... I tried to push him away from Garnet with the paddle. I thought if I could just get her free from him, she'd be okay, and together we'd get Will aboard. I was leaning really far over the side of the boat and I jabbed at him, then I jabbed again. I kept jabbing at him, trying to get him to let go of my sister. But he wouldn't. He wouldn't let go. She was drowning. I didn't know what else to do … so I hit him with the paddle instead. That finally did it. He let go of Garnet and she managed to escape from him, choking and gasping for breath. She grabbed the paddle and I pulled her to the boat and helped her in. Then I held her while she leaned over the side and puked. I was so relieved she was okay, but when I turned back to help Will, he was under the water. And he wasn't moving.

"Garnet and I both jumped in and together, we dragged Will back to the boat. I climbed in and pulled on his arms while she pushed and we finally got him onboard. I remember thinking, 'Good, he's not fighting us, we can save him now.' I didn't know …" He swallowed. "We laid him down on the bottom of the boat, and Garnet bent over him. When she told me he wasn't breathing, I didn't believe it. I went numb. She started CPR and screamed at me to get the boat back — to hurry, get the boat back! So that's what I did. I drove us back, Garnet did CPR and mouth-to-mouth the whole time. As soon as I arrived at our dock, I ran inside and called 911. When the police arrived, they questioned Garnet and she told them she'd been alone with Will on the boat. Because she knew. She knew I killed him. She was trying to protect me."

Nathan and I sat in stunned silence; Garnet's sobs were the only sound.

Finally, Byron said, "Nathan, I'm so sorry. All this time, I've wanted nothing more than to tell you how sorry I am for what I did that day."

"I don't know what to say," Nathan whispered.

"You don't have to say anything. I don't expect you to ever forgive me, but I really wanted you to know the truth. Will's death had nothing to do with witchcraft or devil worship or whatever else you might want to call it. It had to do with me. I panicked. I didn't mean to kill your brother, Nathan, I did what I thought I had to do to save them both." He looked away again, blinking furiously.

Nathan cleared his throat and said, "Up to now, all I really knew about that afternoon was that Will and Garnet were on the boat, Will drowned, and Garnet was going on about some spell she put on him," said Nathan. "Byron, Will died from drowning."

"I know, Nathan, I hit him with —"

Nathan interrupted. "The coroner's report said his death was due to drowning. It referred to the bump on his head, but that wasn't the cause of death. The autopsy report said it was a minor bruising and wouldn't even have knocked him out. That's why they never ended up laying any charges on Garnet. You didn't kill Will, Byron, he drowned."

Byron stared at him, open-mouthed. "I didn't kill him when I hit him with the paddle?"

Nathan shook his head. "No. He drowned. Over the last couple of years, whenever I thought about my brother's accident, I always imagined Garnet watching from the boat, laughing, while my brother died right in front of her. But, according to what you just told me, Garnet didn't watch him drown, she tried to save him, almost drowning herself in the process." He stared at his hands. "And I believe you."

With that, Garnet's sobs grew louder and she threw her arms around both Nathan and Byron and drew them in tightly. I looked away, feeling like an intruder. Finally, she let go of them. Garnet wiped uselessly at her face; black streaks ran from her once heavily lined eyes. They sat for a long moment, emotionally drained.

Nathan broke the silence, "I'm sorry I spread all those rumours about you and your family … and for vandalizing your house. It was like I couldn't control myself; I was so angry …"

"I'm sorry, too," said Garnet. "For everything."

"It's too bad you didn't have this talk a long time ago," I said. "It would have saved you all a lot of grief and agony."

"I guess it took getting stuck together on an island," said Byron. "I'm really glad you had that hunch about the photo, Sarah."

I smiled at him. "So, Nathan, tell us. How *did* you end up here?" I asked. "People have been searching for you for days."

He looked sheepish. "It's my own fault. Chalk it up to one more stupid thing I've done lately. Since Will's birthday, it's been pretty rough at my house, almost as bad as when he first died. He would have turned seventeen, and do you know the really horrible thing? I can't picture him anymore. I'm forgetting him, and I never wanted to do that. I found that old picture of us at the island when I was looking through some of his things after a visit to the cemetery. It used to be our favourite place. So I went back to his grave a few days later and left the picture for him. I thought he might like it. Too bad it didn't make me feel any better.

"My life kept getting more and more out of control. Every time I saw you, Garnet, I'd fly into a blind rage. As for breaking your window? I don't know what got into me. And that wasn't the only time I did something to your house. I was scared of the person I was becoming. So when J.D. showed up at Jack's party Friday night, saying stuff about how you were going to take care of me, I knew that things had gone too far. I'd had it. All day Saturday, I stayed home and wondered if I was going crazy. I didn't answer the phone or go outside or anything. I knew I needed to get away, I needed time to think and sort myself out. Have any of you ever felt like that?" he asked, his face pained.

Byron and Garnet both nodded solemnly.

"Then I remembered the picture I'd left for Will of us at our island. I always felt better there, and suddenly, I knew that's where I had to be. Maybe there, I'd be able to think. So Sunday morning, when my parents headed off to church, I pretended to be too tired to get out of bed. As soon as they left, I packed up some food, grabbed an old blanket to sit on, dragged our canoe out of the boathouse, and headed out. And I was right; I could think there. I had a great day — that is, until the rain hit. I wasn't even halfway home and it was coming down in buckets. Before too long, my canoe was full of water and I could barely paddle, it was so tippy. I managed to get myself to this island and pulled the canoe ashore to wait out the rain. Not easy with that rocky shoreline."

"You mean this isn't even your island?" I asked. I couldn't help but be disappointed that in spite of all our efforts, we still hadn't found the island in the photo.

"This island? No way. Ours is so much nicer," he said. "Anyway, by the time the storm passed, it was getting dark. I was cold and hungry and ready to go home. Little did I know, I was soon going to learn the real meaning of cold and hungry. When I went to launch the canoe, I discovered that it was gone. I guess I didn't pull it ashore far enough and the waves washed it away. It was pretty rough; I should have known better. Too anxious to take cover, I guess. So here I've been ever since. I figured someone would find me sooner or later. And look who showed up! So, when are we going home? I'm dying for a cheeseburger," he said, with a wide grin.

"Let's go now," I suggested, standing up.

"Uh, we have a bit of a problem with that," said Byron.

"Oh, really?" asked Nathan warily.

I frowned. "We ran out of gas just before we got here, but Byron, you can just row us back, right?"

"Sure. If we had both paddles, I could," he said.

"What do you mean?" I asked.

"He means that when we got to the island and you took off before we could secure the boat, Byron ended up wedging one of the paddles between a couple of rocks and it snapped in two," said Garnet. "If he hadn't have been so rushed and worried about you, it wouldn't have happened."

"Oh," I said sheepishly.

"You mean you're stranded out here with me?" asked Nathan, alarmed.

"We're not stranded. We have a boat and one paddle. It's just going to take a little longer than it should to get back," said Byron. "It's getting dark; we'll leave as soon as it gets light."

Nathan put his head down and groaned. "I thought I was going home tonight."

I don't think I've ever felt so bad for someone in my entire life.

Rescue!

Date: Thursday, November 8
Location: An Island Somewhere in Lake Muskoka

The drone of a boat motor roused me from my pre-dawn stupor. We'd been lying around the fire, taking turns keeping it going, but the sound of the distant motor got us immediately to our feet and on the run. I fell at least once, maybe twice. Byron got to the shore first, shouting and waving his arms to get the attention of the people on the passing boat. I was right behind him. Turns out it was an OPP vessel, all lit up like a Christmas tree. What a great present! A searchlight beam swept over us, then back again. Shouts came from the boat. It turned and headed our way.

"Sarah! Stay right where you are!" bellowed a familiar voice through the megaphone.

"Dad!" I shouted. "It's my dad," I told the others. I cupped my hands around my mouth and shouted, "We found Nathan!"

He didn't answer immediately. Then he asked, his voice breaking slightly, "Nathan, are you hurt?"

"No, I'm okay!" he shouted hoarsely.

"There are a lot of people who'll be very relieved to hear that!" Dad boomed. "Are Garnet and Byron Hopper with you?"

"Yes! We're all here!" I yelled.

"Good. We're going to get the boat in position for you to board. This isn't going to be easy!"

He was right. The OPP boat was a lot bigger than the tin boat, so it wasn't able to wedge between the rocks closest to shore. The boat had to be manoeuvred towards the shore sideways, and those waves, while not as strong as when we'd arrived, were still relentless, rocking the big boat and scraping it up against the boulders. An officer in a wetsuit jumped overboard and helped each of us climb over rocks to the waiting boat, where Dad and another officer hoisted us, one by one, up and in. Nathan went first; I went last. We all got more than a little wet while boarding, reminding us how frigid that water was.

Dad gave me a tight hug when I boarded, but otherwise avoided my eyes. I can read him like a book, and I knew that although he was happy and relieved to have found me, he was also angry that I'd been lost in the first place. In other words, I was in deep doo-doo. My only hope was that since we'd found Nathan, I might be able to convince him that the ends justified the means.

"My canoe!" exclaimed Nathan. Sure enough, a canoe had been lashed to the back of the OPP boat.

"We found it while looking for these clowns," said Dad grimly, jerking his thumb towards Byron, Garnet, and me. "And I can't wait to hear your story." Nathan opened his mouth to speak, but Dad held up a hand to stop him. "But I will wait. For now, we'll just get you back." Nathan smiled gratefully as someone wrapped a blanket around him and led him to a seat.

A blanket was draped over my shoulders, and I joined the other three mounds huddled together. The officer in the wetsuit fetched our things, which we'd left at the fire in our haste, while the other officers rigged up the Tin Tippy for towing.

We were going home.

Even though it was the wee hours of the morning, there was a small crowd waiting on the dock when we arrived, including a couple of local reporters. Somehow they'd gotten wind of the dead-of-night rescue. As we jumped out of the boat onto the dock, we were immediately bombarded with questions and flashing lights. Nathan was engulfed in the arms of his parents before being taken away in a waiting ambulance. Garnet and Byron were embraced by their parents. Garnet beamed while answering the reporters' questions. Once I disentangled myself from Mom's bear hug, I hustled over to share the limelight.

I couldn't believe it: We actually found Nathan! We

were heroes!

Finally, Dad broke up the party. He told everyone that we needed to go back to the station and answer *his* questions. Byron and Garnet piled into the back of his car; I took shotgun. I loved any opportunity to ride in the front seat of a cruiser! The Hoppers and my mom planned to follow us in their vehicles. When Dad joined us, he slammed his door shut. I could tell by his grim face that he was furious. After the chaos on the dock, the inside of the car was deafeningly quiet. The look Dad shot me would have cut through steel. Yowza! For the first time ever, I wished I'd sat in the back seat. I hoped that having Byron and Garnet in the car with us would have saved me from a furious rant. It didn't.

"When will you ever learn?" Dad asked, through clenched teeth. This was before we even left the parking lot, by the way. Then he said, "Don't you ever do this again!" followed quickly by "When you get on that bus in the morning, you go to school. You have no business sneaking off somewhere else!" There was more; it actually went on for quite a while. I just sat there, stared out the window, and let him blow off steam. Finally, he stopped. I risked a sideways glance at him and wondered if he was really done. To my utter shock and astonishment, he was blinking furiously. Were those tears? Was my dad, the tough guy, crying? I'd rather get yelled at than see Dad cry.

"Sorry, Dad," I mumbled.

He reached over and put his big hand over mine, grasping it firmly. It stayed there the rest of the way to the station.

Back to Normal?

Date: Friday, November 9
Location: School, Home

Aſter spending yesterday morning at the police station and the rest of the day sleeping, I was back at school today. It felt like I'd been gone for a week. And what a reception I received! People constantly stopped me in the halls to ask questions about finding Nathan. I've never been so popular in my life!

During lunch period, I'd just sat down with Mindi, Stacey, and Cori in the cafeteria when Leanne joined us. "So you were involved in the investigation after all," she said, with a wide smile.

I gave her an apologetic shrug. "Yeah, though not quite as officially as I led you to believe."

"Official enough," she said. "I saw Nathan when he got back from the hospital. He told me everything. Thanks." She leaned over and gave me a tight hug before joining her friends at a different table.

I watched her go and then noticed Cori scowling at

me. Nothing unusual, but to my surprise, so were Mindi and Stacey.

"What?" I asked.

"How could all of this have gone on without any of us knowing about it?" asked Mindi. "I thought we were friends!"

"We are," I said.

"Friends tell each other everything," she said. "I didn't know you were working with the OPP and searching for Nathan. Why didn't you tell me?"

"Like I told you, Mindi, she thinks she's too good for you," mumbled Cori under her breath.

"Sarah?" asked Mindi, her voice up an octave.

"Maybe it's true," I said, crossing my arms.

"What?" Mindi's voice was now a shriek.

"Who told me to just do my project but otherwise stay away from Byron?" I asked. "You were so worried that Byron and I had something *romantic* going on." I rolled my eyes.

"I wasn't … I mean … you still could have told me what you were doing. I would've listened — I did when you told me about Nathan —" protested Mindi. I gave her a warning look. I didn't want anyone to know about him vandalizing the Hoppers' house. That had become ancient history between the Hoppers and the Tremballs. "I would have helped you, Sarah," she insisted, getting the hint.

"Maybe Sarah's right," said Stacey. "We were all too worried about Byron's reputation."

"Seemed like it," I agreed, with a nod. "Oh, and by the way, Cori, thanks for ratting me out."

She looked startled. "What do you mean?"

"I know you phoned my house on Wednesday and told my mom I was ditching school."

Everyone looked at her, and she winced. "How did you ... ?" Then she countered, "It was a good thing I did, though, right? That's the reason you got rescued off that island."

"Oh, sure. Friends always call friends' parents to tell them when they're doing something wrong, right?" I snapped.

"Geez, Cori. Would you call my mom if I skipped school, too?" asked Stacey.

"Why did you do that, Cori? Friends aren't supposed to tell on each other," added Mindi. I wasn't about to remind her that Cori and I weren't exactly friends, so it probably wasn't a good argument.

"I ... uh ..." Cori stammered. I have to admit, I enjoyed watching her get so flustered. "I — I'm s-sorry, Sarah," she finally got out. I'm sure it was literally painful for her to say this.

"Yeah, okay," I said, graciously accepting her apology like the better person I am.

"Sarah ... it wasn't just Cori who talked to your parents," said Mindi sheepishly. "Your mom showed up at school and hunted Roy down. He ended up telling her how Amber was after all that food you had packed in your knapsack, how you were wearing layers of sweaters like you were planning to be outside all day, and how he overheard you saying something to Amber about hunting for an island?"

I grimaced. That snoop! Did I have any privacy?

"He was worried about you!" she claimed, when she saw the anger on my face. "That's the only reason he told."

"Yeah, me too!" said Cori. I snorted.

"Then your mom called your dad," explained Mindi. "He rounded us all up and asked us all sorts of questions. Cori told him about how much time you'd been spending with Byron —"

"Of course," I said, nodding. To my satisfaction, Cori's face reddened slightly.

Mindi continued. "When your dad found out that Garnet and Byron weren't at school either, he called their parents. From there, it didn't take him much longer to figure out that you were all out on the lake in the Hoppers' boat."

"He *is* a detective," I said.

"We were getting really worried when it was taking so long for them to find you," said Mindi, frowning.

"The OPP ended up spending a lot of time searching for us further out on the lake," I explained. "I guess we'd gotten a bit turned around while we were out there, and the island we found Nathan on was closer to home than we realized."

"We're all just really glad they found you," said Mindi. Stacey, and even Cori, nodded in agreement.

Later, in geography class, we were given time to work on our projects. I walked back to Byron's desk. He beamed at me as I approached. It was a facial expression I'd never seen on him before, so I almost didn't recognize him.

"Hi, Sarah," he said. Hey! Social skills! At last!

I smiled back and plunked myself in the seat in front of him. "You look happy. Things going well?"

He grinned. "Things are amazing. You know what Garnet's going to do this weekend?" He paused, giving me time to guess. Of course I had no idea. "She's breaking up with J.D.!" he exclaimed, with a grin.

"Hey! That's great. How will he take it?" I asked.

"How does J.D. take anything?" he answered, shrugging. "I want to be there. Maybe I'll get to kick him out of the house!"

I laughed. "So, where's the hoodie?"

"Oh. I decided not to wear one today," he said. Then he grinned and took out his notes. "Looks like we can finally get working on this project!"

"Oh, joy."

We weren't working for long when we were interrupted by a couple of students asking us about finding Nathan. We ended up talking about our adventure on Lake Muskoka with everybody in the class, including Ms. Lytton.

Byron really seemed to enjoy the attention. He answered questions, smiled, and even laughed. I guess after so many years of people not liking you because of your beliefs, it would be such a relief to have people like you for the right reasons. He's a good guy, whether you agree with his beliefs or not. I hope people will start to see that.

I think they will.

I think there might be some truth to the Law of Three. Take Garnet and Byron: they did a good thing by finding Nathan and now good things are happening back to them. For instance, a truce has finally been reached between them and the Tremballs. And those nasty rumours about the Hoppers are already starting to become a thing of the past.

Then there's Nathan. He vandalized the Hoppers' house and harassed Garnet on a regular basis, and look what happened to him! Stranded on an island. He could have died! Was that the Law of Three? Is that what he got in return for treating the Hoppers so badly?

I'd like to believe that doing good things for others does result in good things coming back to you. Although … it hasn't seemed to work for me. After all, here I am, stuck at home, serving night one of a two-week incarceration. That's right, I'm getting punished for finding Nathan! Garnet and Byron didn't get grounded, did they? They didn't have to endure never-ending lectures from their father about the dangers of detective work, no sirree!

Maybe the police would have found Nathan eventually, but the bottom line was that we found him sooner — thanks to my crazy hunch! I don't care what Dad says, he's never going to change my mind about being a detective. His lectures will just go in one ear and out the other and before I know it, my two weeks will be up. I'll be on the loose again, looking for somewhere else to stick my nose!

One of these days, Dad will appreciate my awesome detective skills.

Acknowledgments

A heartfelt thank you to my critical first readers, Lizann Flatt and Wendy Hogarth, for their ongoing support, valued advice, and friendship. I don't know what I'd do without them.

Thanks to Barry Jowett and Andrea Waters for their enthusiasm, thoughtful critique, and insightful recommendations.

Thanks to all my family and friends who have supported my writing efforts with kind words and positive encouragement.